Fatma

Middle East Literature in Translation

Michael Beard and Adnan Haydar, *Series Editors*

Other titles in the Middle East Literature in Translation series

The Committee
Sonallah Ibrahim; Mary St. Germain and Charlene Constable, trans.

A Cup of Sin: Selected Poems
Simin Behbahani; Farzaneh Milani and Kaveh Safa, trans.

In Search of Walid Masoud: A Novel
Jabra Ibrahim Jabra; Roger Allen and Adnan Haydar, trans.

Three Tales of Love and Death
Out el Kouloub; Nayra Atiya, trans.

Women Without Men: A Novella
Shahrnush Parsipur; Kamran Talattof and Jocelyn Sharlet, trans.

Zanouba: A Novel
Out el Kouloub; Nayra Atiya, trans.

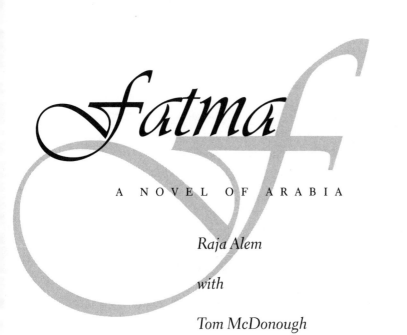

Fatma

A NOVEL OF ARABIA

Raja Alem

with

Tom McDonough

Syracuse University Press

First Paperback Edition 2005
05   06   07   08   09   10   6   5   4   3   2   1

The paper used in this publication meets the minimum requirements
of American National Standard for Information Sciences—Permanence of
Paper for Printed Library Materials, ANSI Z39.48–1984.∞™

Library of Congress Cataloging-in-Publication Data
Ālim, Rajā.
[Fātimah. English]
Fatma : a novel of Arabia / Raja Alem with Tom McDonough.— 1st ed.
    p. cm.—(Middle East literature in translation)
ISBN 0-8156-0738-5 (cloth : alk. paper) 0-8156-0812-8 (pbk. : alk. paper)
I. McDonough, Tom. II. Title. III. Series.
PJ7814.L53 F3813 2002
892'.736—dc21   2002004525

Manufactured in the United States of America

She is dancing on the sea.
There is no shoreline.

She wonders what it would be like to go sailing—
to heaven, perhaps, or to hell. She could fight with
sea monsters, or mate with them. Or sit beside them
on their lightless deep-sea thrones.

Some time ago she grew weary of living her
whole life as a woman. At the invitation of her
mysterious friend, she left her body and journeyed
in the Netherworld where everything was a shadow,
insubstantial yet complete. She was able to travel
thousands of years and thousands of miles in the
blink of an eye. She found out what it was like to hit
the wall of thinking and feeling. Her body took on
the shape and substance of a dream. There were
no walls anymore.

RAJA ALEM is one of the modern Arabic world's most distinguished writers. She is the author of seven novels, as well as many plays and collections of poetry. *Fatma* is the first of her novels to be published in English. Raised in Mecca, Alem now resides in Jidda, in the Kingdom of Saudi Arabia.

TOM MCDONOUGH is a writer and cinematographer. He is the author of a novel, *Virgin with Child*, and a story collection, *Light Years*. He has written for the *New York Times*, the *Chicago Tribune*, and *Premiere*. He was the cinematographer for the Academy Award–winning *Best Boy*.

Contents

Fatma

1 *How Her Story Broke*

There was a blue cast to Sajir's handsomely sculpted lips. He was possessed by blue devils.

Sajir grabbed Fatma by the elbow and yanked her down the dark alley beside the decrepit stone building. They skidded to a halt in front of the trash cans. The porter, a towering Yemenite, stood there with his mouth open.

Fatma loosened her grip on her elegantly embroidered *abaya*. The hooded, shroudlike gown slipped down around her waist. Her hair tumbled to her knees. Her breasts were lovely.

Sajir was panting so hard he could barely get his words out. His wife's beauty infuriated him.

"This woman . . . this woman is a curse!" To make his point to the porter, he grabbed Fatma's arm and twisted it sharply. "Don't you ever, ever let her into this building again. Never!"

He shoved her down the steps at the front of the building. Fatma landed on the street and rolled in the dust.

She sat up immediately, her long hair mashed under her left buttock. She felt nothing—no anger, no humiliation. She was a crumpled black tent with a bit of embroidery on it. Numbness seeped through her arms and her chest. Her heart was frozen, her feet were getting cold.

The stone parapets, ranked like soldiers along the roof, looked down and studied her. There was no traffic this time of night, so the discarded woman was free to sit in the middle of the street as long as she liked. She might have been a broken statue piled on top of the trash that never seemed to get picked up. The Yemenite porter steadied himself and resumed looking at the street with a cool professional eye. He was a kindly old man.

A spark of rage twinkled in the statue's eyes. Fatma got to her feet, left her *abaya* in the street and walked away. The black gown was a cold mask between her and the gaping world. She cast it off without thinking, though she knew that nothing would make her husband more furious than her publicly uncovered body.

The porter picked up the *abaya* and walked after her.

The road was dark, endlessly dismal. Fatma walked on for several minutes before she became aware of the porter trying to drape the *abaya* across her shoulders without touching her, begging her to wear it. He was trembling; the black cloth slithered in his arms like the mysterious creature it was to him. The bright words embroidered on the silk nagged him in a language he did not understand. He could feel their awful power in his bones.

Fatma's spark of defiance faded. She sagged and sighed and with a blindly automatic motion she covered herself. The coolness of the silk sent a shiver through her. She told the porter to go back and leave her alone. He looked over his shoulder, hesitated, then moved away.

Fatma walked toward the lights blazing on the main road. She blinked at the blasts of wind from the cars whooshing by—they were just like the hissing demons that possessed her husband's soul. Suddenly exhausted, she stopped and let the lights wash over her. Twenty years a wife . . . twenty years of marriage, twenty years in prison . . .

she had no idea where to go or what to do. She had no one to turn to. She'd fallen away from everyone she knew, even her father. She'd never had time to cultivate friendships with other women. For twenty years she'd been married to that . . . that poor excuse for a man who kept her a prisoner in that old dump of a house. A year or so ago, when her father died, she'd counted the times she'd seen him over the past twenty years. Three: the day she got married, the day he first got sick, and the day of his funeral.

She thought for a second about Najran, her faraway, faraway homeland. She switched off the image like a too-bright bulb.

The enormous porter was back, following her at a discrete distance, making sure she didn't throw herself under a speeding car. Nothing was further from Fatma's mind. Twenty years of not even setting foot on a dusty street—now she was taking a bath in dust and noise and light, and she was enjoying the rush, the crazy motion.

Very few drivers passed up the chance to honk at a silk-robed woman standing in the middle of the road in the middle of the night. The horns startled her, but she stayed where she was. She tried to study the expressions on the faces of the drivers. They were doll-like, all looking straight ahead as if hypnotized by the same spell. And they wore the same impersonal mask as Sajir when he lowered himself on her and pushed into her.

The Yemenite stood tense as a boulder at the edge of a cliff, watching her with his dark, liquid eyes, waiting for the thump of her body under a car. He was ready to jump, but modesty kept him too far away to have a chance of saving her.

She stood there for an eternity, eyes fixed on the cars, all kinds of cars, especially the red ones, red as the devils that grabbed her when Sajir came to bed wearing that grillwork mask of his. Twenty years, night after night, Fatma faced that mask. Twenty years she fed it, washed its rags and went to bed with it. Twenty years of being treated like a thing, trampled.

A red car whizzed within an inch of her. She looked down at her arms. Her skin was breaking out in red and blue welts, as if Sajir were pouncing on her. She watched the devils creep up her arms. More horns blew. The Yemenite inched closer. He was saying something Fatma couldn't catch.

Then his voice took on a rehearsed tone, strangely soft. He wasn't exactly talking, he was chanting a prayer, a very old prayer used to calm wild animals. The ancient sounds quieted Fatma. The waves of confusion ebbed; she could see things now, not just the lights. She wanted the Yemenite to keep singing. She turned her back on the tooting horns and lifted her face toward his chanting. The bruises faded from her arms. She wanted him to go on praying forever.

"Don't be frightened," he said. "I know a place where you can hide. Come on, get out of the light, get back in the shadows. You're not the sort of woman who . . ."

His words hurt her head. She wanted him to sing his prayer again. But he kept talking in human words.

A car pulled over. A young man got out and strode up to the Yemenite.

"Leave that woman alone, you moron! What do you think you're doing, following a woman on the street?"

The Yemenite dropped back. The young man's shoulders were high and tense as a hawk's; he looked ready to hit.

Fatma was frightened, but she was fascinated by his compact fierceness. Though he was very young, there was something about him that seemed to have woken from a distant time. She felt warmer, and her warmth reached out for him.

He looked at her anxiously. "What is a lady like you doing out on the street at this hour?"

Fatma saw his face clearly for the first time. She was stunned: he was the exact replica of her secret friend, the companion who stood beside her at the stone wash basin. She asked herself if her secret friend was real or a mirage in the desert of her isolation. She no longer knew.

"The lady is not alone," the Yemenite said. "I'm her servant and I am escorting her home." The guard's eyes widened in a plea for confirmation. Fatma was too tongue-tied to do anything but nod.

The young man relaxed. "Well, if you need a ride, I'm at your service."

"No, thanks," the Yemenite said. "A taxi just dropped us. Our house is down this street . . . not far." He took Fatma's elbow and steered her toward the house, leaving the young man staring after them.

A man like that, Fatma could tell what he was thinking. She knew he wanted to be sure they made it home safely. A man like that, a gallant defender of a lady's honor . . . yes, he was the very image of her secret companion, so like the figure on the brass urn in her father's kitchen, the hero holding the lion-flag.

The memory lapped over her, softening her, making her young again. She felt seventeen, fresh, facing life for the first time. Her husband loosened his grip and let go of her. His cold mask faded away. She was seventeen . . .

2 *Her Wedding Night*

She was sixteen. She was thin, dressed all in purple, and her legs were trembling.

She and her father, Mansoor, had no women relatives, and so it fell to him to dress her for this occasion. All through lunch she could feel his distance. It dawned on her that this man, her father, was the last in his line. He was sixty-eight, maybe seventy, but he had actually lived only two or three years of his life. His taste for solitude was so strong that it kept him from living.

The women in Fatma's family outlived the men. Her grandmother, the legendary Shumla, was the queen of longevity. Shumla had lived forever—or long enough, at least, to witness the passing of every man in the family: twelve brothers, thirty uncles, hundreds of cousins, and the dozens of husbands she kept marrying. She'd given birth to a son, Fatma's father, when she was, by conservative estimates, a hundred and fifty years old. The son was utterly devoted to her, even in his dreams. Fatma's father had no interest in women other than his ancient mother.

When he was twenty, Shumla married him off to a friend of hers; the bride was seventy. She died giving birth to Fatma at the age of one hundred. Grandmother Shumla named the child Fatma, meaning

"The Nurturer," or "Nurse" for short—as in, "the one who nursed your own mother right out of this world."

Shumla believed that Fatma was identical, spiritually and physically, to her mother. "That's one mistake I never made," the old woman said, "having a girl. Leave it to a simple little girl like you to destroy one of our long-lived women."

It was only last year that Shumla finally dropped her guard against death. Fatma never understood the passion for life that raged in women like her. Confined to their rooms, hardly ever rising from their beds on the floor, what did they have to live for? Grandmother Shumla was such a battler, though, always able to look death in the eye. This much Fatma did understand: her grandmother enjoyed hearing about men dying. She ruled a kingdom of dead men; she fed on their deaths. Their dying was her solace, her sustenance in an endless, miserable life.

When the family left their tribal home and moved to Mecca, Shumla lost everything she loved. She had no herd to care for anymore, no fields to wander in, only the cagelike rooms of her one-story house.

Every morning she spread out her reddest carpet and held court for the neighboring women. One of the women volunteered to cook for her, another said she'd clean the house—anything to please this regal personage. Shumla told jokes, offered criticism, bestowed compliments, and in general drew out the best in the women. She said whatever crossed her mind without fear of offending her young admirers.

One morning, rather lightheartedly, she announced, "Ezrael, the angel of death, sleeps under my bed. He's always been there, I keep my eye on him. I fool him by marrying strong men."

The woman smiled at the wicked joke. They wanted to be friends with Shumla because they knew that in addition to the angel of death, she also kept a stash of magic cures under her bed. Whenever there was a problem with someone's love life, the old dowager would sit down and mix her magical leaves and powders into a strange-smelling dough. Her potions never failed to purify the heart and other vital organs.

"Nothing should block the passageways of love," Shumla advised. "The fire of love has to burn freely, it has to consume your flesh. Otherwise the fire will go out and you'll lose your lover."

The women gathered closer, famished for her wisdom.

"No matter what," she went on, "never entertain lovers when your organs are sluggish. Because this will make a poor impression and weaken his desire."

Shumla was utterly shameless when it came to discussing the most intimate matters. Concerning the sacred rules of cleanliness she advised, "You don't want anything to spoil the scene, no unwanted odors. So be careful what you eat. Whatever you eat, it should only enhance your pure, natural scent. If you think about what kind of smells your lover likes—not to mention other activities—you'll learn a few things that can be weapons for you. Take advantage of them—vary the use of your weapons. And remember, there are rules of variation. Animals use their instincts to sanctify the earth with their breath and sweat and pee—whatever has the power to mark the soil and tweak its interest. It's no different with you and your partners."

Whereupon she retired to her bed and the company of Ezrael, the angel of death.

One day Shumla entered what she called her "period of purification." She embarked on a fast, subsisting on honey from bees that fed solely on acacia blossoms. After seven days she exuded the fragrance of wild acacias. On the seventh night Ezrael, the angel of death, left her bed. Shumla could not bear to see him go. She got up and walked blindly after him, leaving her headdress behind.

The neighbors found her sitting regally in the crotch of a *nabk* tree looking toward the horizon, toward the great mountains of her homeland. When Fatma saw the contented look on her face, she thought of something her grandmother used to say when sniffing the first breeze of morning: "Smell the acacias. It is the call of the mountains of Shummer."

Mornings and evenings Fatma sat with her grandmother for hours waiting to catch the scent of the acacias. Shumla's cheeks were framed by jet-black curls blowing in the acacia breeze, and the scent of acacia from her own body marched forward to meet the breeze. The mountains of Shummer, she told her granddaughter, rose in the north, far, far away, in two great parallel chains, one called Aja, the other Sulma. Aja and Sulma were famous lovers who had run away from their tribe — Shumla's tribe — only to be captured and killed, then transformed into huge mountains. So the lovers stood, facing one another for all time, singing songs whenever winds or shadows passed over them. The happy look of anticipation on Shumla's face as she told this story was the same expression she wore when entertaining suitors. It was the look of a grand lady destined to reach the land of undying love.

Shumla arranged to leave the world as simply and purely as she'd come into it. The scent of acacia thickened when the neighbors covered her corpse, completely dressed in green, with stone slabs. She was free at last from life's limitations. She took with her all her potions and secret formulas, which increased the feeling of emptiness in her wake. Her ministrations were sorely missed in every lover's bed.

✦   ✦   ✦

Mansoor, Fatma's father, came home after lunch. Fatma's hands were wet with dishwater when she answered the door. Her father stared at them as if their wetness meant they were excessively alive.

"Take a shower." His voice was flat. He seemed relieved just to get the words out.

Fatma could barely control the ironic lift of her lips; he'd never said anything so intimate to her.

"And put something new on," he said. "Something presentable." Now he sounded bored. Fatma was getting interested. "You are old enough to get married," he said. "There's no point in postponing it."

He left.

He returned with a young man whose presence filled the small room despite the fact that he kept looking at his feet.

Fatma had been sitting there for three hours, immaculately clean. She was ready for this scene to end. Whenever she glanced at the young man, who was dressed entirely in white, he looked at the floor. Her father looked at the floor too. Only Fatma, the sixteen-year-old girl, seemed to relish the delicate moment. She liked the idea of sudden, drastic change. Somehow she knew that her fate permitted no truce with life. Little Nurse Fatma, descendant of the Queen of Longevity, was ready to become a bee in the hive.

She glanced at the handsome young man (he had the darkest mustache she'd ever seen) and trembled. The trembling darkened the folds of her purple dress. What were they waiting for? The twilight was dimming. Her skin was getting softer.

There was a knock on the door. Fatma's father exhaled loudly, grateful for the interruption. He turned sharply and signalled his daughter to leave the room: she was to stay in the kitchen while he received the visitor. When she got up to leave, she felt a jolt; the young man was looking at her. She sucked in her stomach and straightened her neck, elevating her breasts. His eyes roamed her body. She turned and faced him. He nearly spilled his drink, but kept looking at her, paralyzed by the quickness of her girl-woman's body. For an endless minute, while her father's back was turned, he stared. Fatma couldn't bring herself to look into his eyes. By the time she got to the kitchen she was shaking.

The voices of three men came clearly from the other room. It was strange to hear voices in the otherwise empty house. One of the men—a sheik—was reciting a marriage contract. The other two voices, her father's and the young man's, were replying as witnesses to the contract.

Fatma sat on a low stool listening to tight knots being tied in her fate. Her gown puddled on the bare concrete floor. She held her head high, but her belly was sinking into the pit of the universe.

For several minutes she listened, though she soon lost track of what the voices were saying. She was concentrating on an old brass urn, the only bit of decoration in the house. The urn was small enough to hold in one hand and it was engraved with images of the Seven Heavens, their skies inlaid with silver knights dancing and fighting in various poses. The half-human-half-bird bodies of the knights made Fatma's cheeks and hands feel warm. All through her girlhood and adolescence they'd been her only friends. For Fatma they were the very embodiment of power. Tenderly, for the last time, she touched them.

They came alive. The tiny urn roared with war cries and shrieks of joy. The knights undulated on the urn, dancing and fighting, moving fast, slowing down, moving faster again, bodies lithe and threatening, pulsing against the bright curtain. The curtain had been there, blinding the window, for as long as Fatma could remember.

She fingered the motes of dust and the sparks hissing in the knights' sweat. When she touched the knights themselves, they flared like lightning; the lightning shot into her. She felt impossibly alive. She smiled hazily and focused on the exquisite figure holding a flag in one hand and a lion's tail in the other. The lion was soaring, cloud-like, above the knights. Fatma had been three years old when it came to her that the flag-bearer's name was Noor. She petted the stretched-out lion with her forefinger.

Her father came into the kitchen. She snapped out of her dream, blushing purple as her dress. Everyone had left, her father said, except her husband-to-be. When she returned to the other room, her fiancé regarded her gravely, as if offended by her dreaminess.

It was Fatma's duty to accompany him to her new home. She moved numbly toward the door of her father's house. Mansoor handed her a wedding gift, a plain black *abaya*. The cowl was so finely woven that for a second she thought her father wanted to please her. But it was only her grandmother's *abaya*; her father was complying with Shumla's wish that the gown be handed down to her granddaughter.

The silk caressed her hands. She was about to inspect the fabric more closely when she realized she had been left alone again. It was her most familiar feeling, this silky solitude; it was her life.

She remembered the *abaya* from the earliest days of her child-hood. It was the most treasured item in her grandmother's wooden trunk. It had never left the bottom of the trunk, never been looked at or touched, never seen the light.

•   •   •

Fatma felt in a vague sort of way that she was a flesh-eating flower, or maybe an animal brimming with energy. Ever since she first became aware of her body, she believed that as soon as she was touched by a man, the animal part of her would spring to life and her inner self would be revealed. She'd been waiting for a sprinkle of rain to shatter her shell and unleash torrents of passion.

She followed her husband down a dusty road, oblivious to the dust and blistering heat. She was light-headed with anticipation of a great transformation, floating along with her eyes on her new life, a life of human contact. She would be changed from a wild and wicked plant into a human wife. Though she shivered in fear of the plant or animal or savage creature inside her, she couldn't stop thinking about all the things she was going to learn about the devil-plant.

She was led to an old one-story house built of the grayest stone she had ever seen. It seemed a suitable fortress for her handsome groom. The house regarded her with the indifference due to a peasant bride wearing a simple purple dress.

She followed her husband into a dark passageway leading to a still darker room. This darkening, she thought, was a preparation for her grand entrance. She came to a heavy door. The door opened and she stepped into a foyer. She was breathing fast. There was a room on the left. The door on the right was closed. There were two other doors in front of her, one leading to a kitchen, the other to a narrow bathroom.

Her husband motioned toward a bed lying on a carpet on the floor. He sat on the edge of the carpet. Then he knelt down fervently, like a man no longer able to hear a sound he'd been listening to. He stared at the blank wall in front of him as if gazing at a terrifying apparition.

Fatma sprawled lazily on the bed—what was he afraid of? She nuzzled his back, warming him. He edged away from her, keeping his eyes on her face, transfixed by its flower-softness. He bent over quickly, as if drawn to her against his will. He kissed her and kissed her again, and again. Fatma slipped into a sea of nameless terrors and pleasures. The world was quaking, her mind was floating away. Her secret self was breathing, swimming toward the surface.

Just as she was reaching out to embrace him, Sajir tore himself away from The Nurse. He pushed her down, jumped on her, spread her legs in the middle of the bed, and split her softness. Fatma froze. He plunged brutally into her, battering the gate of her soul, breaking it open, smashing her tenderness and wrecking the path that led to the face she'd wanted to show him, her true, hidden face.

So the rules were set. Sajir would go on forcing himself on his bride, breaking her, burying her wild flowers under scars and heaps of rage. She could not understand where his rage came from. Could he be the avenging angel of all the men her grandmother had consumed in the heat of her passion to live so long? Had Fatma inherited the ancient dowager's vindictiveness along with her passions? Was she being punished for the old lady's sins?

3   *Untaming the* Abaya

here wasn't much space to move around in. The house amounted to two rooms, one of which she was forbidden to enter. Sajir had left early carrying several bottles filled with liquid in different shades of yellow. He'd made it clear that she was not to go into the east room. She could use only the kitchen, the bathroom, and the room where she'd been crushed last night.

Fatma was not curious about the forbidden room. She had no interest in anything but her dreams. She thought about preparing her grandmother's *abaya* for embroidery. For some time she circled the bedroom aimlessly before taking refuge in the welcoming black silk.

She opened her grandmother's ebony sewing box, the one thing she'd managed to save from the days of her innocence. There were no scissors, but there was plenty of thread in many sizes, though all of it was insistently dark. She separated the dark shades of blue and green from the nearly black shades of blue and green.

The third time she glanced at the forbidden room, her eye caught a flash of silver in the sewing box. She used the silver thread to embroider a circle on the cowl of the *abaya*. The cloth around the circle rippled, reaching out to the needles and thread in the sewing box.

She hesitated about working on the lower part of the gown. Then she came to a sudden decision: the best place to start would be the edges. She would define the borders between black and white and all the other colors. In this way she would limit the kingdom where black, and only black, had reigned for so many years. She stitched a delicate border of letters on the hem, the cuffs and the neckline. The darkest thread she reserved for embroidering a mountainous world teeming with miniature life.

She felt a sting of longing for the old urn. But it was too late for sweet memories. Her pain poured into the ranks of knights on the black mountain of silk. They seemed to be rising, following her fingers.

◆　◆　◆

She was putting quick stitches in the hem when her husband returned and headed straight for the forbidden room. Before she could blink he was inside. She smelled a strange odor. Sajir stepped out of the room, locked the door, and stood next to her. She felt dizzy, she was seeing things.

He wanted her again. She lay down, aware only of the strange odor enveloping her. His sweat had a desperate, blind animal reek. The smell aroused her. She arched toward him. He recoiled, got to his feet and went back to his room.

◆　◆　◆

Over the next few days the room became a nagging mystery for Fatma. She needed to know the source of the peculiar odor.

On the sixth day of her marriage, Fatma's curiosity turned into an unruly demon. The next time her husband opened the door to the forbidden room, she slipped in behind him.

The door opened on hundreds of blank eyes. The eyes were hissing at them. Fatma and Sajir stood speechless. She was looking at a collection of snakes, a whole tribe of them. Dimly, she began to understand that this room was her husband's snake farm. It was crammed with cages large and small, and in the cages were snakes of all colors and sizes, slithering in unimaginable patterns, goggling at her, all of them at once. They stared blankly, as if their eyes were merely decorative, subordinate to other, more accurate senses. Fatma was so spellbound that she didn't feel her husband's anger or hear his hissing when he pushed her out.

Standing in her bedroom, away from the blank-eyed kingdom, she realized that Sajir must be milking the snakes and extracting their venom. She recalled her grandmother's stories about the soothsayer of her old tribe, the wizard who had dedicated his life to taming the untamable, to cultivating the invisible world, rendering tribute to all the worlds, human and otherwise, harvesting remedies for human sickness, and maintaining nature's balance of peace. In the tight circle of the old tribe, all creatures were respected, all had their place in the encampment and the pastureland, all contributed their share to the general well-being.

◆   ◆   ◆

Married afternoons: Fatma sat watching her handsome, ominously distracted husband. Sajir spent most of his time soaking dead rats in a pail of water. The stench overwhelmed the kitchen.

After draining the rats' remains from the pail, Sajir brought in a box of frogs, miserable looking corpses that seemed somehow aware of the indignity of sharing a watery, foul-smelling grave with rats. He stirred the frogs into the rat-broth (they twitched as if startled) and left them to soak. In an hour they became rats in smell and taste. With a satisfied look on his face, Sajir served the snakes their tasty midday meal. Fatma broke out in gooseflesh, shuddering to think what might happen if he decided to turn a human corpse into a giant rat.

But Sajir was concerned only with the medicinal properties of his brew, which he stored in a large gray bottle. Tucked away on a high shelf, the bottle haunted Fatma's dreams. She dreamed about puddles of rat broth, oceans of rat stew. She dreamed that the rat juice was swamping the city and changing everyone into rats—the true objects of her husband's desires. She wondered what would happen if a drop of the liquid fell on her skin. Would she make a nice meal for the staring snakes? Her spine shivered in anticipation; she knew for certain this was going to happen. The vile juice sat on the shelf, lurking like a sinister cloud ready to explode.

It took Sajir seven days to cook enough frogs in his kettle to provide the red and black snakes with the rat juice they required. By the end of the week all the swill had been consumed and it was time to start the soaking ritual again. Every Thursday Sajir started soaking his dead rats again, disguising the frogs in their distilled essence, and replenishing the supply of rat juice.

◆   ◆   ◆

The first time Fatma entered the forbidden room, she had been blinded by the sheer force of life. The feeling was as subtle as it was strong; she'd opened her hands and sensed the radiant power clutching her fingers.

Morning light entered the room from the east. There were windows along the top of the south wall, so the whole day's cycle of light and shadow played itself out in the room. The effect was of a complete universe rising and falling, constantly changing. Fatma sensed that snakes needed this feeling of the planets' movements; they liked the mingling of motions and the exchange of gifts between different sectors of creation.

She never felt alone when she sat in the room, never exiled or excluded. She was surrounded by a small world of tree limbs, rocks, boxes of sand and sawdust, even a miniature swamp. A plump gold snake curled lazily around a large block of quartz, pressing the tiny wrinkles in its pure white belly against the gleaming rock, possessing it. The embrace struck Fatma as so intimate that she had to close her eyes and turn away.

◆ ◆ ◆

Seven nights after Fatma first entered the room, a Great Horned Black escaped from its cage and slithered into bed beside her, moving like satin across her skin. She was delirious with pleasure when she felt its bite. The burning sensation shot deep inside her, and she passed out.

Sajir couldn't be sure if the scream came from his wife or the snake. She cried out only once—something between a shriek and a hiss. He saw the Great Horned Black crawling away from her. It was the deadliest snake in his collection, and the most valuable. Though he knew it had bitten his wife, he couldn't bring himself to kill it. Paralyzed as if bitten himself, he watched in horror as the Black moved back to its cage, gliding, glistening wickedly, leaving a trail of slime and dark droplets that filled the house with the sharp scent of musk and amber, especially in the room where Fatma lay. There the smell seemed very peaceful.

The snake curled up in its cage, drawing its coils tighter and tighter until its blackness seemed about to burst. The scent of amber grew stronger with each twitch of the snake's coils, swelling and tightening the knot of the creature's ferocious passions.

Sajir had seen enough magic for one night. He ran to the cage and snapped the door shut. He was sickeningly aware of the futility of this action. One look in the snake's eyes told him that the snake had the power to escape whenever it chose.

His bride needed looking after. Skilled as he was with venom, Sajir knew that nothing could stop the Horned Black's poison. Fatma was sure to die. No one had ever survived the powerful venom; one drop was enough to kill an elephant.

Sajir felt he had no choice but to disburden himself of the victim. He ran barefoot into the night and didn't stop till he came to the house of Fatma's father. The old man received the news with a numb blink and followed his raving son-in-law back into the night. They arrived at the foot of the bride's bed and stood there sharing their helplessness.

They waited a month for her breathing to stop. At first it was a loud crackling in her chest, then it subsided to a rattling sigh, then a smooth breeze sweeping through her body. The father and the husband felt almost soothed by the breeze. Then Fatma entered a phase they could not fathom: they were unable to tell whether she was dead or alive. She lay there like a ghost, not uttering a sound, not even a sigh. But when they touched her to see if she was getting cold, their movements stirred her and she would start to breathe again, very softly. Then she sank back into some invisible satiny world where she seemed to need no air at all.

The snakes' cages went strangely quiet, as if the wild creatures understood the struggle going on in the bride's body. It was as if they were waiting for the final battle—all except the Great Horned Black, who seemed to be asleep, lost to the world. Or perhaps he was lurking, ready to strike again. The snake looked at once drowsy and dangerously alert. It was watching. It was sinking into its own special darkness, gathering its blackness and concentrating it all on Fatma. Over a considerable distance, through thick stone walls, and through the shadows in the rooms, the snake could sense with reptilian clarity every shiver or blush of warmth in the body of its victim.

Sajir felt a double sadness: he realized he had lost his most precious creature, the source of his most powerful poison. When properly diluted, its venom produced a broad range of medication capable of curing the most pernicious maladies. Undiluted, the venom was death itself. He shuddered to think of the pure poison coursing through his wife's veins. The father shuddered too.

Both men were anxious for Fatma to die. No one was permitted to return from the terrible hell where blindness mated with death. The bride must die, otherwise she would turn into a freak, a changeling whose very existence would constitute an affront to nature. The men pooled their weakness and willed her to die.

She lay serene under the fever's assault. The men felt assured by her pallor; blueness about the lips was a sure sign that the end was near. The blueness spread and darkened. To the men, the changing colors on Fatma's skin were shadows of death's hand. They were torn by conflicted feelings—dark joy mixed with hate and jealousy. They were thrilled by the image of death radiating from the blue hand, but at the same time they hated Fatma for forcing them to stand around interminably and witness her agony.

The fever broke at night. The crescent moon was shining like a knife in the sky, the bride's body was showing incontestable signs of death. She was dark blue, not breathing at all; she was nothing but an evil-looking lump of sapphire sculpture. Mansoor was relieved when his touch failed to stir his daughter. Finally he could go out and make the funeral arrangements.

Sajir was in shock. He spent the night staring into the eyes of the Great Horned Black, which were turning to onyx. But the snake was not there to amuse its breeder in his bewitchment; it was somewhere in the sapphire body of the bride.

The father returned at midnight, panting with the effort of carrying the funeral finery; it hadn't been nearly so much work to marry her off. He doubled a long sheet of white cotton and spread it over her slender form, scattered dried roses in the coffin, fetched a bucket to soak the sprigs of glasswort in, and fumbled in his pocket to be sure he had enough camphor to write God's name on his daughter's forehead. Sajir, who had been watching all this, returned to his disturbingly silent snake. The father was obliged to perform the washing ceremony by himself.

He stood by his dead daughter's feet feeling sick, sweating with sin. He felt in the presence of a curse; he believed that this washing, the act of purification, was somehow sinful. He wondered whether to continue with the ritual or just wrap the changeling corpse and dump it in a ditch behind the house, or bury it and erase all trace of the wicked thing and the evil it contained. It seemed sinful to treat it as human. It was in no way human. It was a bewitched thing lying somewhere in the middle distance between what was human and some other, shocking sort of existence. The distance frightened him. He sensed that to lay hands on the arrangement of his daughter's transition to a world he could not see might cause him to drown in that world.

Yet there was a magnificence to the body stretched out before his eyes, a lethargic beauty in the aura around the deathbed. And the scent of musk was spreading like the mist of life itself, or the memory of an old song, the echo of a once-living woman remembered musically, reviving a life never fully lived.

Suddenly, standing at his daughter's feet, which had turned the darkest shade of blue, Mansoor detected a change in the atmosphere. The air was heaving rhythmically, breathing in time to the music of his daughter's body. He shook himself to get rid of the wicked sensation. He knelt over the body and went ahead with the washing ceremony. Then he froze again, thinking: *This is a bad thing to do. She has been cast beyond the pale, she is no longer a creature worthy of human consideration, she is evil—evil forever and ever. There is no sense thinking otherwise.*

Nevertheless he knelt, trembling. He uncovered his daughter's magnificent sapphire corpse and carried it toward a bare wooden bench. The skin was satiny on his forearms. He felt overwhelmed by the body and laid it down in a hurry. He sprinkled a few drops of glasswort-water on her black hair.

Fatma's sigh came from the depths of creation.

In no time she was sitting up and blooming. Her sapphire skin turned ruby-red, then paled to a rosy glow. Her arms and legs rippled like the limbs of an enchanting nymph, no longer a girl but a seductive woman overflowing with life. She looked around; there was an unmistakable erotic twinkle in her eyes.

When Sajir heard the father's chokes and gasps, he rushed to the washing bench. He was stunned by his wife's voluptuousness. He recognized the sudden awareness of passion in her, but he could not understand it. He glared at her wriggling. The message was clear: she was the most dangerous kind of snake, a woman-snake, and she was about to rise from her coils and strangle him. Sajir summoned his coldness and all his other weapons. He knew that he would have to tame her before he could plant his seed in her. And he would have to be very careful about how he tamed this snake.

◆   ◆   ◆

The next few days brought Sajir more disappointment. Once again his favorite snake escaped from its double-locked cage and crawled into the water basin. The rough stone sink had been sitting at the foot of the east wall for as long as anyone could remember. It was white, square-shaped, set two feet into the floor, and cut from a single block of flint. It seemed always ready to accept a series of sacrifices. In fact, Sajir used it to cremate snakes who were too sick to save. The basin glowed wantonly in the fires, as if happy to feel the burning flesh. And when the fires died, it shone more brightly, having sucked some evil power from the flames.

Sajir studied the Great Horned Black coiled in the middle of the basin. Its skin was showing cracks and fissures. Every morning there was another oozing purple crack. The snake was falling to pieces, erupting from within, its scales and spots loosening and floating in a great dark circle. Clearly the snake was mortally ill, or suicidal. Sajir hoped against hope that it would pull itself together and spare him this terrible loss. The snake was one of a kind. The Great Horned Black figured prominently in occult manuscripts, where it always appeared genderless and without a name. Its venom was a syrup of seven different colors, from each of which many remedies could be concocted. This snake was the source of Sajir's biggest profits.

It had come to him of its own accord, having appeared one night shortly after his sixteenth birthday, just as he was entering puberty. Sajir's father was still alive at the time and eager for his son to carry on his trade of mixing venom. But Sajir proved to be a disappointment. The more his father watched his efforts with the reptiles, the more he felt that the lad lacked the largeness of spirit needed to get the snakes to relax and release their poison. With the arrival of the Great Horned Black in their little house, however, the father changed his mind. The appearance of such a unique and wild creature could only augur well for his son's future. Indeed, a Great Horned Black meant prosperity for the whole family. By the time his father died, Sajir had mastered poison-craft—not in a very creative way, but mastered it he had.

Now the Great Horned Black was leaving him, withholding the favors it used to give so freely. Sajir knew that it was foolish to ignore any sickness in the snakes. Certain diseases were contagious and could infect the entire collection if he failed to take quick and effective action. A mortally ill snake, or a snake who had a mind to kill itself, had to be sacrificed on the spot, burned alive—otherwise the others were likely to follow its morbid lead.

The Great Horned Black continued to deteriorate, sinking deeper and deeper into the shadowy hollow by the east wall, but Sajir kept putting off his final decision. A smell of smoldering amber filled the room, causing him to wince at the thought of incinerating his magical fountain of money. The stench was becoming intolerable. The snake's skin continued to split into infinitely fine pieces, as if waiting for something definitive to happen. The other snakes, repelled by the stench, coiled up as tightly as they could and kept to the shadows. Sajir knew he had to act if he wanted any of them to survive.

The ninth night after Fatma came back to life, the bride sat up in complete silence and stillness. Shortly after midnight, the stench of amber drew her into the snake room. As soon as she crossed the threshold, the stone basin burst into black flames that flickered in the eyes of the snakes and danced on Sajir's sleepy eyelids. He jumped out of bed and saw the whole house pulsing with light and darkness. The scent of musk was soaking into the walls, into every crevice, wiping out the stench of amber, assimilating its power.

The musk was coming from Fatma; her body was saturated with it. From that night on, wherever she moved, the scent of musk was all around her. She was possessed by its perfume; her very flesh seemed a distillation of its mist.

4 *My Captivity*

t first Sajir did everything he could to keep Fatma away from her father, and from life. Then she took charge of the keys to her own cell and began to enjoy her tiny, solitary world. When Sajir got around to suggesting that she pay a visit to her father, she was too preoccupied by her visions to leave them.

She stared at the shadows cast by the snakes and attempted to embroider their fascinating twists and turns on the silk of her *abaya*. As she became more familiar with the shadows, she discovered the art of blindness, the art of living in union with unknowable creatures. In their blindness, the snakes seemed to be reaching out to her.

This seeming blindness was the first thing Sajir had noticed about them, and he had learned how to put their infatuation to good use. Now he put Fatma in charge of his entire eternally twisting collection. It gave him a sense of relief to do this. He felt he'd been waiting all his life for just such a surrender, this shift of power to his wife.

Though he never took the trouble to teach her anything about his exotic creatures, she could sense their needs; the knowledge of what their blind souls wanted seemed to be in her blood. They knew where to move and Fatma knew how to move with them far better than she'd ever known how to be with her husband or father. Sajir was astonished at the way the snakes responded to her voice, even when she fed them meals they didn't like. In all his years of tending to them, Sajir had never been able to get the black-red creatures to eat frogs unless he went through the process of changing them into rats. But with Fatma—here they were eating insects right out of her hand!

◆   ◆   ◆

She began to feel a change in the gossamer membrane covering her brain. The silvery curtain relaxed its hidden folds and the ceiling over her head cleared and suddenly she could see waves endlessly shining and vanishing like rivers running merrily in eight directions all at once, breathing together. Every time a wave appeared there was writing on it, letters or numbers signifying things unknown to human beings. Ordinarily, these things lay buried and unseen, deep beneath the waves of the gelatinous silver curtain covering her mind. Now, to Fatma's senses, the curtain contained billions of kingdoms: each letter or number on the waves was a monarch reigning over millions of exquisitely sensitive rivers, and each river was written in light, a joyfully scented light alive with incredible creatures that dazzled her soul. A glimpse of a letter on the curtain brought the invisible rivers to life; the waters shone with perfumed soldiers whose scent was light itself. Fatma spent all her time deciphering the smallest letters that appeared to her and bringing them under control.

One morning, as she was looking at her husband, his heart and soul opened before her like a book. The vision was so nakedly clear that she had to look away to leave him some privacy. She saw the cobwebs of fear in his muscles, in his sinews, in his blood. He was being held captive by a nameless enemy, a monster. She refrained from tracking the enemy into the depths of his soul. After this nakedness, she resolved never to raise her eyes to him again.

◆　◆　◆

Bit by bit, everything in the small world of Fatma's house became hers. She came to reign over a kaleidoscopic kingdom of poisons, danger, and surpassing, deathless beauty.

She discovered a strange shadow on the side of the flintstone basin. It was shaped like a human body, but the face was featureless. Though she spent several days meditating on the shape, she was unable to persuade it to talk to her.

One night Sajir got furious with her because her hands came too close to his neck. He was sure that a single scratch from her could kill a man—the woman was that poisonous. Several times during the night he opened his eyes only to be blinded by the scent of musk directly under his nose. Then he noticed Fatma's fingers wandering across the pillow toward his neck.

"Get away!" he hissed. "You're poison!"

She got out of bed, leaving a choked silence behind. Her silence infuriated him.

"One scratch from you could drop a camel!" he shouted after her. His belief in the power of his wife's venom was so strong that he started walking around on tiptoes and obsessing about the seven colors racing through her veins.

◆　◆　◆

Fatma spent the rest of the night sitting on the floor of the snake farm staring at the shadow. Suddenly it came to life. She gasped when it took on the shape of Noor, the flag holder of her girlhood. The lion's tail was wrapped around his waist and he was gripping the end of the tail in his hands. Noor himself had the appearance of a snake with a lion's head. Fatma stared at the thick hair covering the lion's head. Was Noor a lion? Or was he one of her husband's snakes?

Like a cloud in a breathless sky, the shape in the basin seemed to want to move away from the wall. Fatma longed to touch it, to merge with the soft, throbbing mystery hypnotizing her, but she didn't want to frighten it away. The image was so fragile that she held her breath for fear of shattering it. It looked at her. She felt like a fish caught and thrown back in the water, breathing only the shadow's darkness. The breath of life was all around her, *in* her, scattered everywhere in next-to-invisible motes that gave her all the air she needed, and more. The shadow's silence seeped into her and she fell asleep on the compassionate sawdust on the floor.

She woke the next morning to a shout from Sajir. He was taking a shower in the bathroom when suddenly the water cut off. He wanted Fatma to bring him some water from the big vat behind the door to the snake farm. This was the vat in which he bred nonpoisonous snakes that had the power of prolonging life. Their skins were blue and spotted with magical patterns of triangles and circles. Sajir was especially fond of bathing in the water from this vat.

Fatma was aware of their power: anyone who touched these snakes would be jolted with electricity. She looked at them churning smoothly at the bottom of the vat. Their current tickled her hands and ran up her arms. For several minutes she drew off the magical water, looking now and then at the faceless shadow in the sink, touching it lightly. Once she poked it to encourage it to take part in what she was doing. She controlled an impulse to walk right up to it and pour some water on it. It seemed to be fading.

Sajir got his water promptly, but he was irritable and kept asking for more, much more than he needed. He stood naked in the shower,

oblivious to his wife. She rarely saw him undressed. He looked so handsome, so finely sculpted—but he seemed to be sculpted from a colorless sort of lead without the least hint of warmth. No matter how powerful the snake-water was, it did nothing for him, and Fatma felt sorry for him. By the time he finished washing, the vat was empty.

She waited all morning for the vat to fill up. When the first few drops began to flow, a bright glaze returned to the blue snakes, and they started writhing in endless circles again.

From then on, the shadow in the sink was pleased to keep appearing to Fatma. It monitored her daily routine and spoke with her regularly about her worries and fears.

◆　◆　◆

A year went by, two years perhaps, or ten—time didn't matter in Fatma's world. She was totally immersed in the snakes' timekeeping: one turn of the tail might mean a lifetime. And a lifetime could be a blink at a flash of the great void they were able to see.

One morning just before sunrise Fatma was observing a dim rainbow in the flint trough when a streak of silver crossed her hair. She lifted her head to its warmth and noticed that the shadow had turned his face away from her.

"It's daylight," she whispered. "Isn't it time for you to vanish, Noor?"

He did not move. He brightened and looked at her.

"Daylight helps make a shadow clear." His speech was a fluttering. "But sometimes it feels better to be vague, without sharp edges."

She stared. "What language are you speaking?" As if to muffle her words, she pulled the silver streak in her hair down to her chin.

"What difference does it make? You understand me well enough."

"Do I sound like you?" She was anxious for a direct answer. "I've never really had the chance to know how I sound. Especially since I got married and stopped talking."

"You speak clearly. Whatever language you speak, whatever sound you make, you're perfectly clear to me."

"I mean, what language am I speaking?"

"I can't help you there," Noor said. "My ears are trained to understand the smallest movement of everything that moves—everything. I hear sounds directly from the great river that every utterance aspires to. There, in the great river, all languages lose their differences and shed their ambiguities; in the great river, all of them speak with the same flowing melody. I'm sorry, but I can't understand words except in this absolute sense."

◆ ◆ ◆

As Fatma spent more time with the shadow, she acquired some of its calmness. Gradually she began to talk freely about her doubts and fears and puzzlement.

"Do you know why my grandmother didn't want to die?" she asked. "All the women in our family fought to hold on to life. And all the men—they couldn't wait to leave. Were the men answering your summons? Why would an immortal shadow like you single out the men and leave the women stubbornly alive? What *are* you—a man or a woman?"

"What difference does it make?" Noor replied, dodging her curiosity about his identity once again. "What is a man? A woman? What are *you*? Why does it matter to you? All you have to do is follow me. You'll arrive at your own conclusions."

"And when I do?" There was a note of sarcasm in her voice. "My sex would have no value?"

"You assume there is a barrier between the sexes. There is no barrier. You will become all sexes. In the end, every creature, every being, will drop its mask and simply be itself—the one self."

"Do you know how old I am?" Fatma asked.

"Old enough to die."

"I can't die," she said, annoyed by his firmness. "I inherited my grandmother's longevity."

"But you just said you don't know how old you are. You could be older than grandmother already."

His mention of her grandmother brought back the old lady's scent, the strong smell of animals and wildflowers that clung to her *abaya* like sewed-on patches. In the days when Shumla was a girl, when she herded sheep on the slopes of Mount Shummer, she used to stuff her headdress with flowers until it became a pillow of basil and red roses. The men of her tribe knew her as the Queen of the Rowanberry Trees. The flowering of the red rowanberries, they said, caused Shumla's sap to rise and made her start looking around for her next husband. Every spring, like a Paschal lamb on its way to slaughter, a new man came to her. All the men dreamed about her, dreamed about taming her body and soul, and in their dreams—and Shumla's dreams, too—she was a civet cat, a wild, musky mongoose.

"My grandmother was a mongoose," Fatma announced with the naïve pride of a child.

"Let me tell you something about men who spend their lives hunting mongooses," Noor replied. "Once upon a time there was a pilgrim guide named King Molkshah the Khawarizme. He had led a caravan of pilgrims halfway to the holy land. As he was returning to his own country, King Molkshah got caught in a storm. Its winds carried the scent of the rarest of rare mongooses and the sands were whipped to the sky by gigantic genii warriors who wanted to inflame the sense of travelers and capture them. The scent of a mongoose is like no other scent—it is sharp and fine and utterly captivating. It crept inside the King and invaded his very soul.

"A gust of wind blew sand in his eyes. It was then that his fate took a drastic turn, because he blinked just long enough to find himself snared by a dream. He got back on his horse and faced into the wind, dreaming of your grandmother. She was galloping behind him like a gazelle. She seized the reins of his steed, who was thundering along like the devil himself. King Molkshah jumped with fright. Yet he felt a thrill at her invasion of him.

"In a flash she jumped on his horse and rode along on its waving mane. The King was so caught up in her scent that he reached forward to throw his arms around her. The horse was flying along and Shumla was shedding her clothes—piece after piece she tossed to the wind till she was totally naked. Then she cast her skin off, too, and showed the King her true body; she was a hybrid nymph and mongoose. She threw herself against his chest and reached behind him, clutching his spine, jolting him with ecstasy. He fainted with pleasure. Her mongoose cry ripped the storm like lightning.

"The courtiers of King Molkshah saw a shining body vanish in the sand. And they saw their King fall off his horse. The courtiers got to him in time to keep him from being trampled, but they couldn't do anything about the taste of the wild animal lingering in his mouth. No one knew whether she was real or a thunderbolt or a hallucination.

"It was at this time that your grandmother Shumla took to wandering. Her rivals among the womenfolk conspired to send her into exile. During one of the tribe's migrations, they left her by the side of the trail to fend for herself. So it was that Shumla began to plot her revenge.

"King Molkshah never recovered from his blinding vision. On his way home he set out in pursuit of the animal that had devoured his soul, and he got lost. Then came news that his heirs had all died; the seven princes, his sons, were found strangled in their beds. King Molkshah ended up sitting naked on a ruined throne, a throne charred like the trunk of a lightning-struck tree. He tried to find comfort in siring a new litter of heirs, but no matter how hard he and his consorts worked at it, his bed remained barren. The wizards informed him that he had been robbed of his seed; he was unlikely to have survivors.

"Following the soothsayers' instructions, the King sat down next to a hollow in the sand and there he saw, in a mist of prayers and incense, his fate being conjured up. In clouds of amber—the clouds were shaped like spirits—he watched the sand heave and shape itself into Shumla. She was radiant, preternaturally beautiful. The storm-dream repeated itself. The King's eyes blazed.

"The seers were standing nearby manipulating their talismans. Just as they had predicted, Shumla turned her back on them. The sand heaved again, reshaping itself into what seemed to be a target of some kind. But the vision was blurry. The King grumbled. One of the wizards stepped forward and swept the sand, clearing a space for the target to emerge. The King's eyes widened. The sand drew itself into fine wisps and drew something on Shumla's back. In the triangle at the base of her spine, in red henna, it sketched hundreds of smaller triangles. There, at the center of the whirling shapes, a little child was nestling.

" 'The oldest triangle is buried here,' one of the seers whispered. 'It is very old, Your Highness, older than the springs of humanity on this earth. It is written that any man who sips from this spring is bound to be impotent. I must advise you, Your Excellency, that your seed has come under attack by the oldest form of siege warfare. Nothing can break through but the arrow of life itself. But once the arrow has broken through, your heir—your one and only heir—will be released from his nesting place.'

"The soothsayer sprinkled more amber about, inciting the mongoose-nymph to address the King directly.

" 'Your heir,' the creature said, 'will indeed be born. But only on top of a minaret built of mongoose bones and hoofs. The birth of your heir and the continuation of your line will be guaranteed only after a mountain of sacrifices has been constructed. You must make a ladder of mongooses disguised as the bodies of women.'

"Obsessed by the need to ensure a successor, King Molkshah hunted down every mongoose and every woman in the vicinity of the pilgrims' trail, spreading death among the women who had conspired against Shumla. With each raid his temple of bones grew taller. King Molkshah hunted like a madman until he had built a shining minaret of hoofs and bones in the middle of the desert. Then one day the temple echoed with the shrieks of childbirth.

"Amid a great clatter of bones, the King's heir galloped down from the top of the minaret. The creature was half-mongoose, half-human. The court historians noted that the year of his birth was also a year of almost universal infertility, since every woman had been hunted down and killed to satisfy the King's mad lust to capture the nymph and guarantee his succession."

"It was a miracle that my grandmother survived the king's lust for revenge," Fatma remarked, "and the massacres."

◆   ◆   ◆

Fatma's body began to change. She was able now to detect the heat of any approaching body. The dimmer the light happened to be, the more sensitive she was. She would sit still and let her senses locate

every object in the house, itemizing them one by one, until finally she reached a state in which her body was able to pass through walls and travel some distance to locate things moving outside. Needless to say, she was also able to identify all the snakes in her husband's vast collection.

She sat alone far into the night, surrounded by their endless, inchoate writhing, trying to achieve the state of blindness in which her body would begin to sink in the musical river, the great invisible river rippling with rhythm and song. She knew that every snake in the menagerie could reach the excruciatingly joyful waters with a mere twitch of its tail.

Whenever she stepped into their room and saw them all, the big ones and the small ones, gliding in their peculiar way, she knew they were swimming in the great river. She had learned to follow the almost imperceptible shivers they used to refresh the shine on their skins and rearrange the patterns on their backs and bellies. One note of the river's music and a snake would instantly change—a new twist elevated the tail, a brilliant square would appear on the nose. The music of the great river had the power to penetrate the surface of living things and tap their source of energy, changing everything about them. It was all so subtle and intoxicating, this intercourse of spirit and flesh.

And when the snakes moved, they invoked the river's music— powerful, puzzling, almost unbearably perfect harmonies beyond the range of human senses—all the more strange because humans, too, were born of the same music and carried its tones and harmonic structure in their blood. It was the music of the universe and it came from the highest frequency, the realm where flesh and spirit were one.

Fatma's blindness became astute enough for her to see that the music was inscribed, quite precisely and formally, in the patterns on the snakes' skin. The small dots were single notes. The triangles, circles, and the ambiguous, cipherlike letters contained the creative essence, the source of the universe. The dome of the earthly sky was but a speck on the skin of one of the larger snakes; the mountains were scales on its vibrating sides. Fatma could sense the shifting of the mountains, their inching along from eon to eon. Her head spun with the music of it. All things—every creature, every object in the world—were merely shadows cast by the musical light dancing from the specks. The music and the light—they were real, like stars shooting into a river of energy, booming and hissing symphonically as they fell. Everything else was an ephemeral partner in this dance, harmonizing for a moment with the inner light, then dissolving and disappearing into the great essence. The snakes were in intimate contact with that essence. Fatma was trying to change her body so that she could achieve the blind suppleness of their gliding and vanish into the dissolving dance.

She sat there all through the night, edging toward the dance, urging each of her senses and the pores of her sadly ordinary skin to succumb to its rhythms.

One night, a thin line of dark blue fringed with wings of silver shot down from her chin, rippled between her breasts, continued down the middle of her belly, right through her navel, and sank out of sight in the dark triangle between her thighs.

Sajir boggled at her. "Get rid of that paint," he said. "Stop acting like a child." He stumbled over the word "child." What he meant, but what he could not bring himself to say, was that his wife was insane.

Later, after Fatma had spent another night swimming in the darkness and the musical light, tiny images developed along the blue line. Sajir could not look at them without getting dizzy. After that, no more lines or images appeared, but Fatma could barely endure the marks of life that had seared her skin and the powerful music that had come to control her. It made her sweat a musky sweat.

5   *When a Neighbor Knocked at My Door*

atma answered the crazy knocking at the door. A shabby-looking woman stood there, raving.

"We're cursed! We're in the blackest black hell! I can't do anything about those lady-crows, nothing can stop them! They're in my dreams! And they're not supposed to be there! I see those black capes of theirs and I break out in a rash — a gray rash! They're eating me alive!"

The woman laughed. A few seconds later she had regained her composure and started speaking to Fatma like an old friend.

"I hate women," she whispered confidentially. "There's too many women! They're everywhere! They're crowding me out of the world."

The woman, who introduced herself as Hasfa, spent the next hour narrating her nightmares in minute detail. As she spoke, millions of nightmare-women swept into the small room. Hasfa's breasts heaved under their weight.

Fatma brought a glass of water to revive her, but Hasfa, who sensed her new friend's stand-offishness, got angry and started talking about her bitterness and agonies all over again. Fatma remained aloof, far away with her blind companions, who were showing signs of restlessness because of all the commotion.

Hasfa was getting no real sympathy, and this piqued her curiosity.

"Would you mind if I took a look at your kitchen?" she asked suddenly. Her eyes fixed instantly on the walls, searching for something.

"*Bism Allah Alyna!*" she cried, invoking God's name with a shudder. "God save us, poor women! Where is it?" She passed her hands searchingly over the walls and waited for an answer.

Fatma realized she hadn't spoken a word since this woman walked into her house. She had a vague notion what she was looking for.

"What about this soot all over the walls?" Hasfa kept asking. She shuddered again, transmitting her chill to Fatma. Then she looked startled, and hissed at her: "It's here, I can feel it! Right here! Where did the poor wife turn into coal? In the bathroom?"

Fatma was stunned. Did this woman have something to do with her dark companion, Noor?

Hasfa didn't give her time to answer. "I can still feel her—the wife running through this room, choking, burning. Can't you wash her away?"

"*Her?*" The question caught in Fatma's throat. She coughed and tried to say something to Hasfa, just one word, but she couldn't. She was overwhelmed by the sound of the single "her."

Hasfa sensed the question Fatma was unable to ask. The woman's babbling energy came back in force.

"Yes, your husband's former wife! She burned to death right here in this kitchen. Sajir was out at the time. They found her splattered on the wall. The firemen had to scrape her off piece by piece."

Fatma heard nothing more. She was watching the shadow on the wall of the stone basin come to life. It did not look like a woman, not one bit.

"That husband of yours," Hasfa was saying, "he's rather difficult to live with, isn't he? You do know what he does for a living, don't you? He's a snake breeder, that one. Well. Did you also know that one of his snakes, one of his pedigreed specimens, was a genii-serpent, and fell in love with him? And forbade him to fall in love with any human woman? I suppose the snake was terribly jealous of the wife, poor thing. It haunted her. When the jealousy got too much for her, she used to come and stay with me. The serpent was after her, she told me herself. Day and night it stalked her. She said it was invisible but it chased her around with fire. The snake was a witch and it turned her house into a living hell. Anything that fell on the floor, it went up in smoke. No cinders, no soot, no nothing—gone! Something landed on the floor—poof!—curtain of fire! Goodbye! It got to the point where nothing could escape the flames unless it was being carried around by a human being. Then it narrowed down only to things that Sajir carried on his shoulder. I guess that's when the serpent's appetite got out of control and it swallowed the wife. Nobody heard a thing— no cries, no smoke. She must have gone up in a flash. When Sajir opened the door he found a body of coal glued to the wall. There was some soot lying around. So you cleaned it off?"

Fatma understood now that Hasfa had come for the sole purpose of telling her this story.

"So just look out for that jealous mistress," Hasfa said. She cocked her head and contemplated the tragedy. Though her story was lengthy and well-rehearsed, it still seemed to take her by surprise.

Hasfa didn't have the slightest idea what was going on at the base of the wall in the other room. The shadow was smiling. Its features were no more defined than before, but Fatma knew from the way Noor was holding his head that the flag holder—or the lion or the snake—was grinning. She could feel his smile spreading around the house.

Hasfa left without getting much satisfaction. The shadow stayed where it was, gazing at the peaceful expression on Fatma's face. She sat down to quiet the beating of her heart. Her pulse slowed, and the calmness of her rhythms spread like a pool, keeping all conflict and noise at bay. Once again her snakes sank back into undisturbed blindness until finally every one of them was basking happily in the tide of her serenity. Fatma, at rest and feeling content, became alert.

"What are you?" she asked. "Genii or human?"

"What are *you*?" The voice Noor used was a whisper so forceful that it shook the air all through the house.

Fatma shivered; this was the first time a real feeling had entered her. Enjoying the shiver, she let it spread over her, all over her, and she tasted its sweet pain. She came very close to discovering the darkness in herself, a darkness as dark as her friend on the wall. She winced.

"You keep trying to capture me," Noor said, "to understand me according to the cages people invent when they set limits on themselves. Man, woman. Old, young. Human, genii . . ."

"Maybe all I want is to get hold of something in you that I can touch," Fatma said. "But maybe you think it's just a feeble attempt to un-charm you."

"Un-charm me? Don't worry, that's not so easy. Let me tell you another story about your grandmother. No one—no human, I mean—really knows if it's true or not. But the story contains the secret of your grandmother's longevity."

"I think the old lady had many, many secrets."

"You may be right about that. In any case, here's the story: Once upon a time Shumla disappeared. Every man in the tribe felt his pride had been injured because they all thought of her as their future bride or raid-prize. Each of them believed that her honor was his to defend. The gossips whispered naughty secrets about her disappearance; kind-hearted people simply said she'd been kidnapped. The most experienced trackers were called in and paid exorbitant fees. The expeditionary raids turned up no trace of her. She couldn't be found.

"Three years later Shumla turned up skipping across the tribe's pasture. She seemed more light-hearted—and even wilier in the ways of snaring men's hearts. Three years she'd been gone, and still the stories about her rang through the warriors' campfire nights. No matter how long the enchantress stayed away, she remained a vivid presence. Shumla was unforgettable.

"Her old lovers set out after her in hot pursuit. Evidently they forgot all about her disappearance—which would have been enough to ruin any woman's reputation, not to mention any chance of marriage. Shumla herself never passed up an opportunity to talk about her adventures. And she told some very strange stories: she had been kidnapped, she said, by Satan.

"This version of Shumla's adventures spread through all the tribes in the desert. She let it be known that Satan, along with a few thousand of his demons, each of whom ruled over a thousand or so magicians, happened to come across her while she was out walking one day. The Evil One invited her to his throne room.

"People got very excited. Soon her story was immortalized in drawings on all the rock faces of the mountains. The pictures were said to have been drawn by agents of Satan. They illustrated Shumla's story in outlandish tableaux: Shumla dueling with Satan, Shumla baffling Satan with cryptic verses, Shumla overpowering Satan with the sharpness of her wit, Shumla forcing Satan to lose his temper, Satan ordering his demons to tie her up and carry her off to his throne room, where she was held captive for three years.

"Satan was usually drawn in purple, in weird poses, contorted in all kinds of heart-pounding struggles—or paying homage to Shumla, or forcing himself on her in his thousand ruby-thrones, all of his thrones at once, hellfire flashing with every thrust. Boulder after boulder was carved, painted, and glazed with images of the insatiable Satan grinding into Shumla and planting his seed in her womb. The final scenes had a somewhat lighter touch: the happy couple, reconciled, embracing under waterfalls of satin which burst into flames, concluding the story with the most charming spectacle.

"The subsequent birth of their offspring was recorded in tableaux of a more mystical nature. The birth was attended by the ugliest imaginable ogresses, painted in gaudy colors. They were shown taking possession of a green, feathery infant. The child was a mighty spirit, born of Satan's indomitable passion and Shumla's equally indomitable inner strength.

"Immediately after it was born, the child was carried off on the wings of demons to the remotest corner of the Arabian Peninsula, where he was nursed in secret caves by desert nymphs. He grew up to be the most powerful spirit in the Peninsula. It was his fate to await the birth of the River Lar, which would bring about the re-creation of the Earthly Paradise.

"Having given birth to Satan's most powerful son—and enemy—Shumla was generously rewarded by Satan himself. Meaning that she was allowed to fight one last battle with her kidnapper. He permitted her to overpower him and escape back to her tribe.

"The green feathery child lived on for thousands of years, worshiping the Almighty in splendid solitude and acquiring the essence of knowledge from the desert's many secret hearts, drawing wisdom and strength directly from its veins.

"Shumla told her story over and over, sketching pictures of it on every dune or rock she passed. 'My son,' she told everyone, 'will appear some day soon. He'll be riding the crest of the great River Lar, the greatest and most fertile river known to man. When the Earth is in its final throes, when all creatures are about to perish of thirst and violence — that's when you'll see my son coming.'

"The result was that every traveler who got lost in the desert expected to meet the green feathered spirit. He lived forever in people's dreams and stories."

"So my grandmother was one of a kind?" Fatma said breathlessly.

While she was listening to the story, without thinking about what she was doing, she had been embroidering pictures identical to the ones her grandmother Shumla had drawn on the desert's rocks. And the pictures were all in green, her grandmother's color.

Noor was struck by how vividly the drawings stood out against the pitch-black fabric of her *abaya*.

◆   ◆   ◆

Fatma fetched pitchers of water for Sajir's morning bath. The water splashed on her dress, pasting it on her curves. Sajir glanced at her thighs. The energy in them seemed lethal, and it made him angry. Fatma handed him a pitcher. He stood there staring at her without taking it. She held the pitcher out to him, but he turned away. Fatma set the pitcher on the floor and walked out.

When Sajir came out of the bathroom Fatma was sitting down, busy with her needle and threads. She looked up at him towering over her, evaluating her body. She let his resentment drip on her like chilly syrup.

"Can't you see the irony of your situation?" he said sharply. "Your body, that body of yours, it's barren as a stone — and there you sit making yourself even more miserable embroidering those idiotic talismans." He glared at the blue line running down from her chin. "You're wasting your time on nonsense; it's not getting you any-

where." He sucked in a deep breath. "You must hate yourself very much."

Fatma closed herself to his last remark; Noor drew a heavy curtain over her ears. She stood up and looked at Sajir. His face was twisted. A deathlike haze clouded his handsome features, there were deep wrinkles around his mouth, and his eyes . . . she'd never seen eyes so dry; they squeaked. She felt sorry for her husband's ruined fineness.

Her pity angered him all the more. He turned, stomped on her purple wedding dress, and headed for the door, kicking things out of his way.

"That's the most hideous dress anyone ever got married in," he shouted. "Look at it. Look at *you*. A pretty picture, isn't it? Leave it to you to find a way to look common."

◆   ◆   ◆

Noor, the shadowy lion-snake, took a great interest in every twist of the tale Fatma was telling with her embroidery; he even directed her stitches.

One night she discovered that all her threads had turned a breathtakingly intense shade of black. It was as if her serpentine companions had soaked her sewing kit in their transformative venom. Or perhaps they were hatching something in the dark shadows of the stone wash basin.

Fatma smiled and gave herself over to their quivering; the lines of her embroidery writhed and sparkled and twined around one another just like the snakes. Noor sat watching the mingling of threads and fingers into a single, shining, black life zigzagging across her *abaya*. As he cast his shadow on the patterns, they shaped themselves into a

paradoxical darkness of fire and silence until the silk of Fatma's gown
was drenched with a liquid in which male and female merged.

Noor encouraged her to put more of herself into her world of
writhing creatures. "Your body is a collection of poems and spells," he
said. "Leave nothing out. Your eyebrows, your lips, your navel—they
are all doors to The Invisible."

"Eyebrows? What's the point of eyebrows on a woman like me?"

"You never know. Eyebrows could lead nowhere—or everywhere.
Maybe they lead to the Kingdom of Blackness. Follow the lines.
Every line has a charm all its own. You'll find your way."

"I would like to find a kingdom—the kingdom I lost when I
turned sixteen, or before. I was a queen then, and the road of life went
on forever. Will I ever be a queen again?"

"Once a queen, always a queen. And don't forget that I'll always
be one of your soldiers, your flag holder."

She was amused. She was also terrified, afraid to believe him. "All
right then. So I am the queen of queens, the owner of the keys of creation." She threaded a needle with a strand of her hair, stitched a tiny
knot in the silk of the *abaya,* and mock-seriously held it up for Noor
to see. "Look, loyal flag holder—in this little knot I've tied up the cus-
todian of the master keys. Its name is Be and its guardian is Aleph. I
hope you'll never, never invoke those names behind my back."

"Oh no, Your Majesty. I remain your faithful servant."

"And you will always be faithful to me, even on the dangerous
roads to your home in the Netherworld?"

"Oh yes. One day I will read you a poem about the road to my
home."

♦　♦　♦

While Fatma was attending her father's funeral, she discovered that the urn had vanished without a trace. She wondered if her father had thrown it out or if the urn and the flag holder had left of their own accord. In any case, they had sunk into the fiery darkness from which they'd come. She felt like a queen robbed of her kingdom.

Dressed entirely in black, Fatma gazed at her father's body all covered in white. Several men, strangers, were milling around in preparation for the washing ceremony. Sajir stood among them, and he looked strange too. One of the men uncovered her father's face so that Fatma, who he imagined was terrified, could have one last look.

She was not terrified; she felt nothing at all. Alive or dead, her father's face looked the same, displayed the same indifference, the same coldness and detachment. He might have been even more aloof when alive.

The men paced around with the restlessness of people doing a favor for a stranger. They were anxious to get on with the ceremony and to bring their ordeal to an end. Fatma kept busy carrying buckets of water from the kitchen to the room where the body lay. The thick smell of lotus hung everywhere.

The man in charge of the washing intoned, "May there be no fear or misery on the road to your eternity . . ."

The prayer struck Fatma as preposterous. Her father had never felt fear or pain; how could anyone expect him to feel anything now? She wanted to go up to the man washing her father's dead arms and ask, "What makes you think your prayers and promises mean anything to this corpse? Do you imagine that death is something new to him?"

She was smiling when the coffin was carried out on the shoulders of seven strangers, and she was smiling when Sajir took her arm to accompany her home. Her smile infuriated him. For days after her father's death — marked by Fatma's smile as an inconsequential event in a family line that was as good as extinct—Sajir refused even to look at her.

•   •   •

Shortly after her father's death, Fatma broached the subject of the burned wife.

"The fire didn't start in the kitchen," she said. "So what burned her?"

The question surprised Fatma as much as it did Sajir. It hadn't crossed her mind at all till the moment she came out with it. Sajir fell silent, shocked. He tried to look through Fatma to see how and when she could have found out about the fire and his former wife. He glared at her for what seemed forever, furiously trying to dig behind her eyes.

•   •   •

Late one night Fatma woke up to find Sajir staring at the ceiling with one eye. It was not that the other eye was closed—both eyes seemed to have crossed the bridge of his nose and pooled into one great eye fixed on the nothingness of the ceiling.

Sajir noticed her wakefulness.

"That father of yours," he said hoarsely, "he's better off dead. He never did anything right in his life, not a single thing. He couldn't even manage to raise his simpleminded daughter. It's incredible what a simpleton he was himself, letting you watch him, letting you see whatever was going on."

Fatma was not provoked by this swipe at her father; as far as she was concerned, he might as well never have existed. But she wanted to be fair.

"He never told me anything about the fire," she said.

This was too much for Sajir. He turned around and bent over her, straddling her without touching her, focusing his fury on the body beneath him.

"No, he didn't tell you anything! Because it was impossible for him to talk straight to you. You're a liar. You open your mouth, the air gets dizzy."

"Our upstairs neighbor knocked on the door last month. She came in and told me the whole story."

Her mention of the neighbor made Sajir even angrier. "What neighbor?! This whole rotten building has been deserted for years—ever since you set foot in it and invited those crazy friends of yours in. Panic swept through the place like wildfire. Everybody left, nobody wanted to rent a room. I'm the only one left, I'm the only one who can stand being around you." He glared down at her. Her forehead hurt.

"What am I supposed to think?" he went on. "That my dead wife paid you a visit? That she complained about being burned up in a fire that couldn't have happened? That some worthless woman wants justice?"

Fatma was wondering where the woman *had* come from.

"This is your problem," Sajir said. "You created your ghosts, you live with them."

◆　◆　◆

In the morning Fatma had many questions for Noor.

"What was the fire trying to do with that woman? Was she trespassing on your shadow-land? Was she really the first victim? *Was* there a first victim?"

Sajir had gotten out of bed and left the house first thing in the morning. He was doing his best to punish Fatma and freeze her out.

He must be wandering around like a homeless person, she

thought; people are probably feeling sorry for him. As a matter of fact she was feeling sorry for him herself, and she had been for some time. Even the house was rejecting him. Her presence and her domination of the snake farm had driven the neighbors away, and now her husband.

Fatma had never discussed the feelings between Sajir and herself, not even with Noor. She'd kept this particular chilliness to herself. She'd always been able to shed it by immersing herself in her exciting work with the snakes.

"Do you think he's going to get rid of me?" she asked now. "I don't have anywhere to go, nobody to turn to."

"He wants to get rid of you, but he won't," Noor said. "Not until your time has run its course in his schedule."

"What are you talking about?"

"I mean this is your place, Your Majesty. The snakes are your subjects—and wise subjects they are—including me, your flag holder. It would take a revolution to topple you from your throne. Don't ever forget that."

◆　　◆　　◆

"I want you to come with me," the shadow said in its haunting voice.

"Where?" Fatma thrilled to the feeling of flight.

"To a land in this book." He showed her a book, but she wasn't able to make sense of its title. She'd never liked reading, she was more or less illiterate.

The letters gleamed on the page, changing into the shapes of living creatures.

"What if my husband follows me and brings me back?" she asked, thinking out loud.

"No one would ever choose to go down this road," Noor said firmly.

"What road?"

"Death."

The shadow spent the rest of the night reading to her about the land in the book, "a land whose gates are made of basil. The gates arch high into the sky, above the horizon. There are many beds in this land, and they are floating on air. If anyone falls out of bed, he falls and falls and falls—falls for a thousand springtimes—before landing on earth." He brought out another book. "The same land," he said, "is also in this book."

The book was blurry because it was the Book of Dreams. Fatma could not fathom it. Noor read aloud and when he had finished she felt possessed by it, as if possessed by a breeze. She fell asleep and dreamed of the land in the book.

She was walking on endless balconies and huge soaring bridges. Creatures made of light walked along with her; birds—messengers, perhaps—accompanied her. They had wings—three, four, eight wings. She'd never seen such lively birds. One of the most beautiful ones flapped its numberless wings, raised a flute to its beak, and blew a terrifying tune. Sajir appeared, dancing to the flute. Fatma's heart swelled with sadness and expectation.

Noor stayed with her through every twist and turn in her dream, reading the secret signs. "Bridges and balconies . . ." he began. "Let us start with the setting of the dream, because it will show us where your body wants to go."

He cited the words of Ibn Seren, the legendary author of the Book of Dreams: "The surrounding walls are your kingdom, your world. The soaring bridges and the balconies are your weapons, your soldiers, your means of escape. Though you feel quite helpless, you are in fact well protected by these soldiers. They are feared, even in the invisible world, with all its might and towering force.

"Light is the most significant feature of your dream. This is a sign which should not be ignored. It is a message and it tells us that in the light, there lies your eventual triumph as a queen, a queen who will escape from the empty pit you find yourself in. The light is the gift of sight, and it is promised to you and your blind subjects.

"Along the way to the throne of ultimate vision and power there is also much trouble and suffering. But Venus is watching every step you take, and you have loyal supporters who can carry you through."

Noor flipped the pages of the dream book to the chapter on Flying Creatures. When he came to "bird," the word shattered in Fatma's face. A flock of birds flew across the page, and in their gliding she saw a message. Their faces were not at all like the faces of birds. Clearly they were angels in disguise carrying a message of victory to those who were oppressed.

"Keep moving," Noor said in a soothing voice. "Never look back or your wings will disappear. The winged creature playing the flute is the angel Esrafeal. His appearance signifies the revelation of a date; it is also an invitation to journey into The Invisible. No human being can afford to ignore a single note from this flute. Those who dance to its tune lead the march of the dead on their way down the road to darkness. So you, Fatma, have been chosen—though not to join the dance. Your paths, yours and Sajir's, are destined to separate."

Fatma couldn't be sure if Noor was being serious or teasing her with melodrama. She went along with his playful profundities without troubling herself about what he really had in mind. All she cared about was his attention. She wanted their conversation to go on and on, no matter where it led.

"This is like a fairy tale," she whispered, "not a serious warning."

Noor vanished, leaving the image of Ezrael, the angel of death, on the stone basin.

Fatma concentrated on Ezrael's flute, trying to get it to play its terrifying tune. She listened for it all night long.

Angered by the deathlike quiet, Sajir came into the snake farm looking for her. When he saw her bent over the basin, he felt the urge to yank her away from it and kick her out of his life.

"My father never told me about these things," he muttered. "This snake woman is a curse. Her body is the quietest trap in the world, but when it snaps shut, that's the end, it's death."

Sajir went on talking to himself in this vein for some time, but he took no action, not yet.

◆   ◆   ◆

Friday night Noor was back, positioned where the angel of death had been. The shadow looked questioningly at Fatma, who'd been worrying herself so thin she was almost transparent.

"I heard the tune of the flute," she said. "It's still running through me. My blood is cold, I'm shaking. It feels like something's cracking inside me."

"What you heard was only a faint echo of the flute's powerful tune. No living creature could survive the real thing. Only once, at the end of time, will the tune be revealed to human senses. Its sound will send us all to the next stage—immortality. All kinds of Hells and Heavens are braided into the tail of that tune."

"I can feel the force of its flames," Fatma said. "The flames look green. How long do you think my body will be able to stand all this pleasure and pain? It's tearing me apart."

"You can stand it as long as you stay well enough to hold on to the charnel house of your body. Dreams are only paths to what lies beyond the charnel house, to What Is Everywhere."

Noor brought out the Book of the Soul and began to read:

"The soul, the queen of light, is reluctant to leave its white pastures; it fights to stay where it is. Winged shepherds watch over it, gently but firmly guiding it. When bones begin to form in the embryo, the soul makes its grand entrance into the body. The dough of flesh and blood rises. The soul enters the body reluctantly, but once she's inside, inhabiting the temple, she gradually undergoes profound changes. The temple is changed too; the separation between the temple and the light that dwells within becomes less. Flesh and bone come closer to the soul; the soul leaves its white pasture lands behind and forgets them. The white pastures are never far away, though; they keep waiting for the soul's great emergence.

"The soul is dragged along by the temple's needs, and grows accustomed to its limitations and mundane desires. The soul loses her original shape, casts off her lofty aspirations, and falls in the dust; gets dirty and turns cold. At the same time the temple of the body becomes less dull and raises its sights to match those of its queen, the ethereal spirit within.

"After some time, because the temple of bones fulfills the queen's need for wholeness, she gets used to it. After all the giving and taking between body and soul, the queen develops a deep attachment to the temple. The giving and taking continues. Finally the temple begins to show signs of decay. The queen is shocked to see the body crumbling, to see it begin to sag and disintegrate. She's frightened out of her wits. She sinks into melancholy and tells herself that it would be a noble thing to save the temple by fighting off the attacks of time and the assaults of decay. But the laws of self-destruction, or self-decay, are immutable. Yet the queen fights against them, and this distracts her from her original task of finding the Light and ascending to her throne in the kingdom of eternal fulfillment. The queen tries even harder to merge with her ruined temple; she wants to stay married to it, she wants to move the ruins to other temples, or other kingdoms. It is hard for her to know which way to turn—should she take the spiritual path or should she live a life of indulgence?"

Fatma searched for signs of deterioration in the time-immune shadow. Finding none, she ran her fingers across her forehead and the backs of her hands. Her skin felt smooth as a snake's, no wrinkles at all. She sighed with relief.

"Snakes are good competition," she said. The shadow seemed amused. "Do you think there's even a small chance," she asked, "that our souls could ask for a way out of the body? The flesh hangs on for so long. Are we doomed to sink deeper and deeper into the shadows we call our bodies, and stay caged in matter forever? Our bodies seem so good at tempting our souls to renew the temple, and the temple is made of such lovely, soft material. And the skin of a snake, it seems to be the ideal bait to lure a soul. Don't you think?"

"The skin of a snake and the shadows cast by snakes are a smooth means of escape, I can tell you that, my queen. As for your own temple, what you see when you look in the mirror is the pinnacle of perfection achieved by a queen, by a masterful soul. You must remember that the snake's art of shedding one's skin every year runs in your blood. When the times comes, your body will be so supple you won't believe how easily it slips away."

She challenged him with her eyes. "Do you think I'm just pretending to be this stupid?" Deep anger was rising in her voice. She truly wanted an answer, wanted to know how he saw her. She wanted most of all to be sure that she *was* seen, that she existed.

"I see you as the ideal companion on any road," he said. "To heaven, to hell, to pleasure or pain. I'd love to escort you, my queen, whichever way you choose to go."

She regarded him with awe. She wanted to tell him how she felt about him, wanted to thank him by saying, "You really do know what I want to hear." But she checked herself, smiled regally, and bowed.

"You are commissioned as an officer of our court," she said. "And you may sail on our ship."

They both laughed. The snakes wriggled to their merry rhythm. Noor returned to his Book of the Soul.

"Permit me to use this book to introduce you to your innermost feelings. The surface feelings are not the ones to rely on, not in our situation. Let us try to reach the senses that work when you're sleeping. When you're dreaming your senses are dimmed, but you can still smell, taste, touch and hear quite clearly; these senses are still at work inside you.

"The body we take on when we're dreaming is immortal. We can fall off a mountain without getting hurt, we can pass through fire unscathed, we can die and be resurrected in the wink of an eye. In no time at all we can go from disaster to triumph—that's what dreams are about, and it's a source of strength we mustn't ignore just because we'd rather be awake."

"But tell me," said Fatma, "which is real, dreaming or waking? Which state is the child of the other? Should we go on sleeping forever? Should we get rid of our bodies?"

"It's not a question of getting rid of our bodies, not at all. Our bodies are the same when we're dreaming, only made of a much more basic substance—light. The closer we can get our bodies to the light, the nearer they come to immortality. What we must do is get our bodies, our temples, to a state of transparency. We must get them to glow. We can do this by believing in such a state and by believing in our ability to achieve it. The great seekers and travelers simply let their senses take charge; they allowed the light within them to aspire. And so they were able to journey across the earth and through the heavens in a single night."

Noor went on to instruct Fatma in how to reach a state where she would be able to meet the Guardian of Visions, the angel who ruled the kingdom of dreams.

"The very best part of you," he was reading again, "and only the best part, is capable of meeting the Guardian. Listen to your dreams, try to follow the rhythms of silence and peacefulness. You will find the Guardian. He stands with his back turned to the visible world, waiting to receive the pages our fates are written on. He stands ready to gather up the awareness of things, the knowledge scattered all around. The Guardian knows—he has been taught these things—he knows our names, our triumphs, our failures. He has a complete description of everything each of us is going to do along the road of life. Our fates and our characters are laid out before his eyes in distinct lines stretching from birth to death. He sees our hopes and hesitations at each point on the curves. He sees it all clearly, he doesn't mix the lines up, doesn't overlook a single one of our quirks.

"The Guardian of Visions works day and night to understand the puzzling signs and symbols in our fate-lines. He rearranges them into scenes and feeds them to our dreams. The sheet on which he reads our fates is a page from the Mother of All Books, where our fates were written long before we were born. The page is inscribed in letters of light which our eyes cannot follow or comprehend. It is the Guardian who reads and revises the fates written in our dreams. It takes all our patience and insight to understand the hints and prophecies in our dreams."

Then Noor set about teaching Fatma how to read. He held out a new book and asked her to shut her senses, to deafen her ears and close her eyes. He pressed her fingers lightly against the page. The letters shed their silence and revealed their meaning. She began to read fluently, following the stories of sleep, moving through the Book of Dreams.

"When someone sleeps, as Ibn al-Qaem has said, there appears a ladder or a drift, a spiral current, for the soul to climb on and leave the body and travel wherever it chooses, in any of the eight directions of Creation. As long as the current moves, sleep carries the sleeper along. But when the current returns to its tomb in the body, sleep vanishes, the sleeper wakes up.

"Certain visionary masters had the ability to see these currents and visualize them as sun rays falling on sleepers from the sky, or as glorious tunnels full of light in the midst of darkness. Sometimes they saw the currents as sunlight splashing all around. The soul joins the blazing waters and drifts in the currents, leaving its visible body behind. The soul's substance is invisible, but there are many pathways of light going between the visible and invisible."

Fatma's inner senses took over; she was beginning to feel free of her limitations. As she became accustomed to using her intuition, she was able to close her eyes and shut out the chaos bombarding her ears and skin, and then she was able to reach the most remote corner of the desert and touch the fluttering tamarisk blossoms and feel the yearning of wandering lovers and hear the twitching of starfish on the floor of the Indian Ocean, in the darkest depths of all seas. The scents of desert creatures reached her, and she drew nourishment from their rough force. She followed the paths of windblown dunes, saw their peaks shifting, saw pebbles tumbling into crevasses, vanishing softly, their whispers echoing joyfully in her heart. She felt everything with alarming vividness, even the quivering of insects sipping beads of dew from the leaves. She could see the invisible tracks left by all creatures (the tracks of insects had a special glow).

When she went back to work in the snake farm, she could sense things crossing the carpet in the other room. She knew what bug was dipping its feelers in the bath water and which bees were pollinating the briefly-blooming flowers on the windowsill.

Fatma's new talents frightened her. She tried to shut herself off; she didn't want to see too many secrets.

Noticing her clumsy efforts to hobble herself, Noor moved to take her further along the inner path. He began by reminding her about the lesson learned by the prophet Abraham in his encounter with fire: "If you were to match your inner fire against any fire lit in the visible world, you'd see that no flame could burn you. The fiercest fire burns within."

Fatma tried quietly to reach the horrifying inferno within. She made use of her long-practiced talent for slowing her pulse and reaching a hypnotic, near-death state so that her spirit could approach the source of heat, the dark maw opening inside her. As her body grew cold, she noticed a river of black flames running up her back from the base of her spine. She could not touch the flames or control them; they remained shrouded, like blazing larvae crawling upwards. She reached down behind her back, trying to touch the tail of the fire. When she came close to it, a pointy black tongue flared and licked her left shoulder blade. She fainted and fell into a black hole.

The pain was like no other pain. It was as if her skin had been peeled off and she was naked, tumbling into a freezing, bottomless pit. She broke out in gooseflesh and shuddered violently. Naked, skinless for eternity, she quaked with spasm after spasm of pleasure and pain. This motionless hell was more terrible than the thousand gaudy infernos she'd been through before.

Finally the pit of freezing fire sealed itself. She felt a sort of peace and was able to move about, though she remained rigid with terror. There was a dark burn mark on her left shoulder blade. It appeared at first to be a mole, but it spread, burning. The heat inside the dark spot rendered every other fire heatless. She struck a match and touched it to the mole. The mole extinguished the flame.

Fatma drew back in horror. This concluded her adventures with inner fire and the flame-larva, for the time being.

6 *The Angry Birds in Her Bed*

It began suddenly one Saturday night. Startled out of his sleep, Sajir sat up and stared into the darkness trying to locate the grating sound of the bird or insect on the loose. When he looked down he saw that it was Fatma grinding her teeth. Stiffly, he lay back and gazed in astonishment at the persistent movement of her chin. Her jawbones were grinding out an awful song.

He called her name. She woke, the song died. Sajir relaxed, turned his back to her and resumed his deep sleep, leaving her awake. After a while Fatma's eyelids drooped and she drifted again into the same grinding song, louder now. Sajir bolted up again and leaned into her face, breathing hard. She woke up.

Sajir measured his anger carefully. "You're grinding your teeth again. How do you expect me to get any sleep?"

She left the bed quietly and sat down by the edge of the stone wash basin. She stayed there until the rays of dawn made a rainbow on the west side of the stone.

From that night on, their bedroom was filled with the shrill song of Vengeance Birds, as Sajir called them, since they made it impossible for him to sleep. He tied a bridle on Fatma's jaw, but her grinding soon loosened it and released the Vengeance Birds, shooing Sajir out of the bedroom and forcing him to sleep in the tiny alcove.

The Saturday after it began, the song changed pitch. It happened just as the sun was moving toward its first throne in Capricorn and the moon was in the Bow. The solitude of Fatma's bed incited the spirits of Saturn. Suddenly, out of nowhere, the bedroom filled with an evil-smelling incense, a mix of mastic, myrrh and African rue. The mist crept adoringly over Fatma's sleeping body, decorating her with hazy images of towers and ladders.

She arched her back, lifting her belly. Dark pathways opened up, reaching skyward from her body. Figures on the pathways cast lovely shadows—soldiers dressed in green uniforms and brilliant metal gleamed in every corner of the room, casting red shadows. The dull jangle of metal studs and iron crowns and the rattle of bracelets and anklets joined the chorus of Vengeance Birds. A cold metallic glow coated the house and oozed through the walls. The spirits of Saturn flashed their weapons and erected barricades of green mirrors that echoed the song's sullen anger. Green figures and red shapes hopped and jingled all around Fatma, their clashing multiplied by the mirrors. The sounds and colors of her sleep speckled the whole neighborhood like the icy droppings of phantom birds.

Sajir stalked around like a wild man; there was no sleep to be had in this house, not one wink. He tried stuffing mud in his ears, but the song insisted on penetrating his very pores. The clatter of iron swords, the jangling bracelets, the everlasting din—nothing could silence the uproar.

◆　◆　◆

One night Sajir came home carrying a water trough the size and shape of a coffin. He set it down near the bed, filled it with water and ordered Fatma to sleep there, floating. One of Sajir's friends had advised him that water was a magic element and that dousing a woman with water was the surest way to put an end to her moaning, however deep its origins. Water, the friend insisted, would silence the whips that provoked the wife's intolerable singing.

The water did put an end to the racket on the perfumed pathways, and the road used by Saturn's soldiers was cut. They stopped running up and down and finally disappeared, as did the noise of their weapons and metal jewelry. The singing died quickly, the echoes in the neighborhood faded.

The moment things settled down, Sajir was seized by blind rage. He felt utterly defeated by the heedless attack of the helpless woman whose husband he had the misfortune to be. He regarded the incident as a show of strength on Fatma's part; that was obvious from the energized rippling of the water she was sleeping in. He began to see her as a forbidden island in the middle of a sea spiked by thunderbolts. (She was rolling around in the water now as if it were her natural element.) The problem, as Sajir understood it, was that water enhanced the transmission of light. And no energy could be more powerful than that of fire dissolved in water.

As for Noor, he was delighted with this turn of events.

Sajir spent a restless night watching his wife's soft body dissolve in liquefied fire. The snakes, with their peculiar blindness, could see his anger. Their spirit-shapes hovered around their queen, watching and waiting for the slightest move on the part of the outside world. Unable to decipher their dripping shapes and symbols, Sajir was aware only of the blue line floating down the length of Fatma's body, writhing right before his eyes, groping blindly along her limbs. The line seemed to contain blue demons, and even some thunderbolts.

During waking hours Fatma behaved like a woman possessed, spending most of her time embroidering the waves of liquid fire on the neckline of her *abaya* and stitching their strange currents in looping patterns that seemed to clutch at her.

Sajir got no rest until he summoned the courage to dispose of the water-coffin. Once he managed to do this, Fatma was naked to his advances. She made no comment about the disappearance of her bed of water and simply resumed sleeping on the hard bed on the hard floor. She took comfort in memories of the waves still running through her. She endured her hours of isolation by listening to the sound of the waves she was stitching in the black silk. The waves took some of the chill out of her limbs.

There was no visible evidence of Saturn's soldiers except for the iron anklet Fatma wore on her left foot. It was a plain circle with a large square clasp on which Saturn's insignia was engraved. The insignia was a black figure wearing robes of dark yellow and green, with even darker shadows. Saturn's limbs were adorned with iron weapons and jewelry that branched into the folds of his robe. His face was hidden. He stood in the middle of a court surrounded by demons and ogres, each one casting an image of its face on the master's figure, transforming him into one horrifying shape after another. The demon's faces were too ugly and various to keep track of.

Though the anklet looked extremely heavy, Fatma strolled around as if it had always been part of her. In fact she moved so swiftly that Sajir couldn't be sure if the iron anklet with the demon-soldiers was there at all. So he stopped paying attention to what his wife was wearing and put Saturn's insignia out of his mind.

Noor understood, with resignation, that the insignia was the Stamp of Suffering, but he said nothing about this to Fatma for fear of alarming her.

◆　◆　◆

Many winters and summers went by during which Fatma and Sajir said not a word to one another. All that passed between them was the silent business of milking snake venom and concocting a vast store of ancient, magical remedies.

One Friday evening in autumn Sajir noticed a delegation of snakes gathering in his farm. Among them he spotted the snake known as Looks Can Kill (one glance from the blank eyes of this reptile was enough to kill a man). Also prominent in the delegation was the King Snake, whose hot belly scalded whatever it slithered over. No vegetation could grow near the King Snake's nest; no animal could enter its field of vision without withering. It could also kill by whistling, and was capable of dropping a soldier an arrow's length away.

Sajir was concerned for his own safety. The only thing that took his mind off the vicious King was one of the other snakes in the delegation: the Praiser, an exceptionally lovely specimen whose presence in the farm never ceased to astonish him. The Praiser had sixty thousand wings, each wing had sixty thousand tongues, and each tongue spoke the praises of the Father of All Names. Since knowledge of this Name meant possessing the power to re-create the world, it was known only to a select few.

The delegation of three snakes—Looks Can Kill, The King, and the Praiser—was surrounded by many kinds of servant snakes, all of them slithering silently within the confines of the farm. As if to clear a space for the serpents' deliberations, a strange scent rose from the snake farm, forcing Sajir to abandon the premises and go outside.

Late that night the snakes became more agitated. They writhed up the walls of the farm and onto the ceiling, arranging themselves in patterns prescribed by the Praiser.

Fatma sat on the bare floor in the middle of the farm and looked up at the center of the ceiling, focusing on the spot where the Praiser had positioned himself, the epicenter from which all the other snakes radiated in head-to-tail lines covering the entire room, including the walls. A waterfall of serpents, a curtain of life, blanketed the farm. The snakes' purpose—praise, adoration—was evident in the verticality of their formation and their increasingly vigorous twitching. As they approached a state of frenzy, steam rose from their eyes and fell as mist in front of Fatma's knees. The mist gathered itself into a ball the size of a camel's eye and rolled around, gaining size and substance till it became a bottle with a stopper stuck firmly in its mouth.

The instant Fatma grabbed the bottle, the delegation disappeared. As she turned it over and over, its heat diminished. Finally she was able to close her hands around it. The belly of the bottle was arranged in twelve coils tightly twisted into one another, in the manner of mating snakes. Fatma's inner eye saw clearly through its glassy skin.

Sajir spent the night wandering the streets. When he drifted back to the snake farm the next day, he was surprised to find the treacherous delegation gone. Fatma showed him the bottle. He examined the twelve ridges on its belly and recognized them from drawings he'd seen in his father's library of antique books about poison. He understood immediately that the bottle contained twelve poisonous springs. Once every ten years the springs spouted twelve varieties of curative vapors. Properly mixed, the vapors had the power to cure any known illness. One sniff could cure a sore throat or laryngitis; it could mend neurological disorders, restore speech to the dumb, sight to the blind, sanity to the insane. A crazy person had only to lean his head into the vapor and his jigsawed brain would be recast with dies of wisdom and common sense.

Sajir was too overwhelmed by this precious windfall to say anything, or even keep it around the house. He carried the bottle at once to the sheik in charge of commerce and was rewarded with a fabulous amount of gold.

Sajir wanted nothing to do with the bottle's healing powers; somehow he had lost all ambition. All he wanted was to follow the road of least resistance, to get as far away as possible from people and the world of the living. He had become a loner, an outsider repelled by human contact, sick of the softness of human flesh and mortal hearts.

◆   ◆   ◆

The air of avoidance and neglect between Fatma and Sajir stagnated until, early one summer, he began hovering around her with a bewildered look on his face. She moved toward him, but said nothing.

"News of my rare snakes has reached a prince in the southwest," he said. "The Prince sent a messenger. The messenger suggested that we tour the countryside and put on shows with our acrobatic snakes."

Fatma's lips parted with amusement. This was the first genuine smile she'd ever shown Sajir, and he was instantly smitten, dumbstruck. She gave in to her smile and let it widen, lightening the rest of her face.

"They asked me to take the collection on the road," he said, recovering enough to repeat himself. "In broad daylight—for curiosity seekers to gawk at."

Fatma arched an eyebrow. Her contribution to the conversation didn't satisfy Sajir's need for . . . for what, she couldn't tell. She was thinking about the destination he'd mentioned, the southwest. She was thinking about Najran, the kingdom of snakes, the ancient walled city that had appeared to her in a dream when she was only ten years old. Her grandmother had warned her never to tell anyone about this dream—"not one word, my pretty one." Fatma had buried her vision of the city and the lovely white pastureland surrounding it: endless fields of white grass, white trees, shepherds dressed all in white, white mountains, white rocks—all reflecting the glory of the kingdom's reptiles, the gorgeously colored Kings Snakes gliding between the walls, twisting on the arches, nesting on top of the columns.

"Wouldn't that affect their milking?" Sajir asked. "Moving them around, I mean."

He had no idea what Fatma was thinking, and Fatma, for her part, knew that he wasn't really worried about potential milking problems. Something else was on his mind. She gazed at him quietly until he calmed down.

Finally Sajir came out with what was really bothering him: "I mean—out in the open, would they obey me?"

◆   ◆   ◆

They were on the road, riding along in a large truck. The cargo area had been converted into a sizable cage for the snake collection and for Fatma, who was disguised in boy's clothing in order to pass as a helper. Most of her face was covered by a green mask—"to protect him in case the snakes lose their temper," was Sajir's explanation for the appearance of a masked boy who stayed with the snakes twenty-four hours a day, squatting right in the middle of them in the back of the truck.

The truck was, in effect, an enormous traveling cage fortified against trespass or escape; the only openings were shafts of light and shadow cast by the grating over the cargo area. The snakes reared their heads toward the flickering sun, drawing energy from it and arranging themselves peacefully, bedding down in the ever-changing patterns of light and dark, which seemed to invigorate them.

During the first hours of the trip, Fatma was blinded by the glare, deafened by the roar of traffic, and disoriented by the novel sense of being tossed around in wide open spaces. She couldn't bear the clamor and coarseness of things in the world. She tried to soothe her nerves by shutting herself down; she fastened the mask over her eyes and ears, hunkered down in the shadows, and kept to the darkest corner of the cage. Still she could not shake the feeling of being swallowed by a terrible vastness, of tumbling endlessly in chaos, of skidding across the bumpy surface of creation. When night fell she was able to remove the green mask, but she kept her eyes shut tight and her head down. At daybreak she retied the mask and crawled back into the shadows.

The third night of the trip, having persuaded herself that darkness provided shelter from the threatening vastness, she loosened the mask, opened her eyes a bit, and looked out. When the sun rose she replaced the mask and retreated to the shadows. She urged herself to accept the raw nakedness of what she was seeing and hearing. But she couldn't sleep; everything seemed to be rushing at her, nipping at her, even changing the way she smelled.

At the foot of a mountain chain known as the Sarwats, they ran into a storm. The winds lashed Fatma like mad whips, forcing her to breathe in gulps. She dove into the tangle of her blank-eyed companions, wrapping herself in their warmth and softness, camouflaging herself in the animals' fear. She sank deeper, like a delicate little worm, into the mass of snakes, hoping to discover, in the symbol-patterns on their hides, some response to the stormy void, to the frenzied maw of the universe.

She spent more than a week buried in the snakes. As the truck climbed higher, the air became thinner and the vegetation increased. She shed her old shivering skin and began to acquire something less vulnerable, more suitable for traveling. She became used to the naked rudeness of things, to the rhythmic jouncing of the truck, to the swaying, and to the sudden mysterious cries she kept hearing. Her new skin was a shield, and it was a pale shade of green.

At one of their stops Sajir recalled her existence. He unlocked the cage and waited for her to stand up, but she stayed where she was, determined not to expose herself to curious eyes. She stared into the glaring sunlight so full of voices and cringed away from the eyes she felt looking at her. She could not bear to look back at them, so she shut her eyes and locked the cage.

The next time Sajir stopped and remembered his helper-boy, Fatma was able to wander outside a bit, though she kept her eyes fixed on the ground. The ground felt steady; it was the only thing that gave her a feeling of stability and peace.

Sajir told anyone who inquired that his helper was a mute, and somewhat touched in the head. This explanation kept anyone from trying to communicate with Fatma, and they were able to proceed without incident.

When she grew accustomed to things and became able to look people in the eye, she was disturbed by the emptiness she saw in their faces. People seemed so caught up by the noise of the world, so hungry to feed on its confusion. Close to the cities, their emptiness was more pronounced; higher up, in rural areas, people were more relaxed. The few humans Fatma encountered on the mountain roads seemed more real than the ones who lived in crowded buildings. By the end of the third week, she came to feel at ease with the festive gatherings that greeted their truck at every stop. Fatma and Sajir were the Prince's guests and everyone was eager to host them.

As they headed further south, she peeked through the chinks in the truck's tailgate and watched the road racing away. From where she sat, with her back to the driver, everything flashed by in glints and shards—houses, people, mountains, cattle. For the first time she felt separate from these things. She understood that this was the purpose of the trip, to cut the umbilical cord so she could look on life from a distance. She peeked out and saluted the receding world, retrieving shreds of energy from it and storing within herself little signs of its feeble efforts to reach the Unreachable. The light and shadows falling on the world followed her like courtiers; the sun, the moon, and the blackness of the night sky nipped at her heels wherever she moved. No matter which way she turned or what corner of the truck she tucked herself away in, the light and the shadows were there, blanketing her. Such was her first exposure to the outside world, and perhaps her last.

Whenever they entered a village, crowds came out to meet them. People looked inquisitively at the helper-boy peering through his mask and tried to catch a glimpse of his face, which they assumed was disfigured. The boy's eyes shone hypnotically, drawing villagers to the snake shows almost against their will.

The snakes didn't have to do very much to entertain the crowds; they just lay there. Once in a great while they stretched out or wriggled a little; everyone gasped and gawked. Now and then one of the village sheiks would request a special performance. On these rare occasions the acrobats were required to do something amazing. Fatma would sit off to the side, playing the inscrutable veiled fakir while Sajir put his acrobats through their paces. The snakes kept their eyes on Fatma, tuning their secret senses to her every whim and shift of feeling, ready to obey her unspoken commands. One time, three Blacks with white horns showed off their talent for changing shape. Following Fatma's orders, they tangled themselves into a tall braid, rose up like the trunk of a tree, and swayed their great horned heads back and forth like flowering branches.

"*Bism Allah al-Rahman al-Raheem!*" the crowd gasped, invoking the Almighty's name to sanctify their astonishment at seeing the snakes rise as one body and shape themselves into a black fountain.

The serpents relaxed their bulging muscles and oozed back down to earth, releasing pools of black water that ran between the onlookers' toes, causing them to scatter. In their panic, people scrambled up boulders and climbed trees. When the hysteria subsided, the sheik ordered Sajir to leave town. The truck hurried off toward Najran, to the dream city.

◆　◆　◆

Fatma was traveling with Noor, her shadow. The night before their departure, she had approached the stone water basin, summoned all her courage, and pressed the black silk of her *abaya* against the wall, making sure that she got a good impression of the shadow before lifting the *abaya* away. The next morning Sajir paused by the basin, whose walls had repulsed all previous attempts at cleaning. He blinked in amazement at the absence of the shadow but left without making a fuss. He didn't want to stir things up or jeopardize the morning's uneasy truce.

Noor kept Fatma company during the entire trip. Wherever they stopped to sleep, in the truck or in a tent or by the side of a stone wall, she spread out her *abaya* and made sure that Noor was shining and sending his vibrations to her bed before she dozed off.

The trip introduced Fatma to life, to roads she'd never dreamed of crossing and faces she'd never imagined existed. She came to the conclusion that she treasured her solitude. She valued her writhing

friends and their blind willingness to teach her the secret pathways to beauty and peace, all the while acting the part of her faithful servants in public, obeying her commands, and making people catch their breath in wonder. The villagers were fascinated by her. She had entered a world where people worshiped her, a world of mesmerized onlookers who stared as if dimly aware of her true sex, and conscious, too, of the great animal lurking inside her, an animal always ready to pounce and paralyze.

The cage got ready to move again and leave everything behind. Fatma and Sajir set out for Najran, the green oasis bordering the Rub' al-Khali, the wasteland known as the Empty Quarter, a forbidden ocean of sand where massive dunes closed possessively over their treasure-horde of strange creatures and killed anyone who dared cross their waves—everyone but the nomadic tribes who were privy to their secrets.

Fatma and Sajir approached the ancient village of Najran and its towering rectangular castles. The thickness of the walls was so intimidating that husband and wife were blind to their flamboyant ornamentation. The crenellations on the turrets stood like soldiers straining to touch the clouds. The ancient houses were surrounded by walls of their own, granting the central edifice the privilege of rising above the others like a private prayer. The main building stood eight or nine stories high. Its ceiling beams were trunks of great palm trees. The walls were compacted of mud and palm fiber, and the windows, which were stark-white, whiter than the dust and the ruins strewn about the hills, stood out sharply against the baked mud. Everything was white—door frames, parapets, the land itself.

Fatma basked in the buildings' warm, rough welcome, but nothing in her experience or Sajir's prepared them for the hospitality of the inner chambers, especially the welcome they received in the house of the Sheik of the Yami (for so the rustic villagers were called).

The Sheik proclaimed an evening of celebration for these emissaries of the Prince. His home was drenched in bold, gay colors: the high walls were painted green halfway to the ceiling, which was pure white, and bordered by sprays of triangles in yellow, red and violet arranged in striking patterns that formed protective spells. The staircase was painted yellow, and edged with red and green. The only decorations near the white ceiling were narrow stained-glass windows, whose light fell like tassels on people in conversation, illuminating their faces with colorful clues about their true intentions and splashing a flood of colors on the floor. Fatma thought she was paddling across a raging river or a rainbow.

The Sheik accompanied them to the roof, where a lavish banquet had been laid out. Dinner was served. Bright palm mats were set on fine red carpets to receive lamb shanks fringed with all kinds of fruit. Fatma shuffled to her place, amazed at the soldierlike crenellations all around the roof. Surrounded by the white soldiers, squinting at the torchlight, she ate her first meal in public.

Everyone ate together—there was no division between master and servant. Fatma ate from behind her mask, but no one looked curiously at her; everyone showed the utmost respect for guests of the Sheik.

Afterwards the servants hurried in with fresh dates and coffee of a gold-green hue. The Sheik ordered drums to be set up around the fire that had been lit on the adjoining roof, only an arm's length away. The musicians tightened their drumheads by the heat of the fire and started playing *al-Razfa*, a twirling dance performed exclusively by men. The beat of the drums, the clouds of incense, the aroma of the

coffee and its trickling gleams summoned up memories of the cara-
vans that used to pass through Najran carrying precious ambergris
north out of Yemen. Many years ago, amber had been a commodity
more valuable than gold, and fierce battles had been fought over
right-of-ways through places like Najran. Nowadays the inhabitants
burned incense to relive their days of glory; the men danced and sang
songs of ancient loves and glorious wars. Only when the sky began to
lighten were the fires allowed to rest. Fatma sat back, dazzled by a
beauty beyond her ability to name. Nothing she had seen in the outside world had prepared her for the brilliance of life in Najran.

The next day, the Sheik of the Yami dispatched his courier with
an invitation for the Prince's messengers to spend some time in his
encampment. Fatma and Sajir and their guides rode most of the day,
venturing into the Empty Quarter, leaving the green oasis far behind.
She was amazed to find herself mounted on a graceful white camel
who craned his long neck to look at her whenever they paused at the
foot of a dune, and blinked his long lashes as if inspecting her soul
when they stopped to plan their way up an impossibly high crag. She
was shaking with the life force she felt between her legs, trembling
with fear that the camel would abandon her. This was her first encounter with warm-blooded animal vitality; she discovered a nobility
in it that carried her higher than the enormous dunes they were
climbing. She looked down, hypnotized, as the beast clopped over
rocks and sand-swept roads and glided over endless salt flats. She lost
herself in the waves of heat lapping at her waist, then higher, at the
back of her neck.

They went far into the desert, farther even than rocks dared to go.
All signs of life vanished. They ended up surrounded by a sea of silky-
fine reddish-gold sand. Sajir sat bolt upright on his mount, nervously
alert.

They rode on into the blood-red sunset and came at last to the camp of the Yamis. Little children wearing silver amulets over their black robes trailed after them; girls with jangling anklets darted across the trail carrying leather waterbags that dribbled and sizzled on the sand; young men holstered their intricately carved daggers, hitched their gaudy sarongs, and scampered after the white racing camels the Yami were famous for breeding. Shepherds eyed the new arrivals, then resumed milking the reddish-brown she-camels. The camels looked up too, shuffled their feet in little dance steps, and went back to giving milk. Masked women put down the bags of goats' milk they were churning, raised upturned palms to their lips, let out long joyful trills, and teasingly evaluated the male guests.

The travelers pushed on, leaving the camp and setting out along a route where no footprints could be seen, which increased Sajir's nervousness. They were making their way by instinct now, trying to maintain a sense of direction in a landscape that had become a sea of labyrinths.

They came upon the Sheik's hunting tent, where a huge celebration was in progress. Fatma was thrilled at the size of the encampment. The tent, supported by fifty poles, stretched long and low in sand so intensely red it seemed to glow. The roof of the tent, a cheerful checkerboard of orange and brown squares, towered over dozens of white-robed huntsmen; for a second Fatma thought she was looking at inverted knights on an upside-down chess board. The bright yellow walls of the tent flapped mildly in the fading twilight. The red sand was covered with redder carpets. Fatma dismounted and stood on what she thought was a river of blood.

Rifle shots announced the travelers' arrival. They were escorted to the Sheik, who rose graciously from damask cushions to greet them.

Tonight was a night of music. No one was immune to the pulse of the drums, not even the camels and goats, and certainly not Fatma's snakes, who slithered into the pools of dancing people and animals. Even the falcons, those invincible silver-masked hunters, danced with the royal huntsmen. The falcons were a sign of the Sheik's power and eminence—thoroughbreds all, lords of the sky, as graceful as they were skilled. Every tribe in the region knew the reputation of these famous birds. The Sheik had embellished their masks with diamonds, and he had been astute enough to enlist the services of the legendary falcon trainer Ibn Sakran, who was reputed to have worked for King Nasra, ruler of the kingdom of reptiles. Ibn Sakran had a talent for tempting wild falcons from the sky and coaxing them to perch on the Sheik's quiver.

Moonlight silhouetted the celebrants, turning everyone into columns edged with gold. Fatma, like the falcons, was masked. From where she was sitting, the people, the snakes, and the falcons bore a pleasing resemblance to one another. Her snakes, who recognized Ibn Sakran and sensed his connection to the King of Reptiles, raised their heads toward the falcons and eyed them like old friends.

The old trainer was sitting on a mound of the reddest sand surrounded by his masked flock. One by one he sent the falcons to the dance floor, and when the drums heated up Ibn Sakran himself joined in, swaying to the pagan rhythms with a falcon on each forefinger, the trainer twirling face downward, the falcons looking up, mesmerized by the night sky—then flipping positions: the master's face swimming in the sky, the masked faces pointing at the rising-falling ground, all of them whirling like the wind.

The dance captured a part of Fatma's soul no dance had ever touched; it was more like a drug or magic potion than a dance. The dancers were floating on air. It seemed she could reach out and touch the spirits the old trainer was taming and hear the strange cries issuing from his flock, the sacred calls rippling across the passive dunes. Incense and steam from the coffee drifted over the sand, casting faint shadows on the talismans carved on buried rocks and bringing to life the ghosts of long-vanished jackals, antelopes, oryxes, ostriches, white camels, and red camels. The stallions snorted.

When the dance came to an end, the falcons on Ibn Sakran's fingers quivered as if in their death throes. The audience shuddered, Fatma's backbone twitched. The trainer fell to the ground unconscious, his warrior-birds fluttering around him. Revived by a cup of musk-water, he returned to his seat on the sand.

Ibn Madhy, the Sheik's favorite storyteller, had been sitting next to his chief improvising verses to the music. When the music died he went on reciting an epic in praise of the tribe's ancestors, summoning the nights of their glorious past to join in this night of celebration.

Stimulated by the dance, the Empty Quarter began to rise, threatening to engulf the great tent. At the stroke of midnight, as the camp was settling into the most sacred time of night, the sand erupted. Out of nowhere, a mighty warrior emerged along with his warhorse. Man and horse took shape in a dark wind and galloped wildly through the camp, casting black clouds over the dancers.

The Sheik jumped up to welcome the knight, who introduced himself as Taray, the Sheik's own brother. Taray demonstrated the power of his name—it signified storm-tossed sand—by dancing like the wind. The entire camp was transfixed by the storm of Taray's whirling; it was impossible for even the most agile fighters in the Sheik's guard to keep up with the way he blended with the shadows and merged with the colors blazing in the camp—the rivers of orange, brown, yellow, and bloody red overflowing on the sand. The colors left their savage stamp on the wind and the dancing faces, and streamed away into the thirsty shadows, trickling into the darkness, pagan colors tinting pagan dancers and drawing the attention of warriors from the Invisible Tribes.

Taray stepped out of the circle of dancers and sat down just to the right of the Sheik. He stared into the desert's darkness as if watching another dance on another, invisible dance floor. From time to time he teased Ibn Madhy by improvising a poem. The storyteller responded with verses of his own and soon the night air was swollen by a torrent of poetry, loudly sung.

Taray edged closer to the fire and raised his eyes to its glow. Somewhere in the distance a shadow moved. Taray stiffened and threw a hard look in Fatma's direction. His eyes tugged at her and she was drawn to him, to something she saw under the embers in his eyes, a sense of recognition, a naked call.

For the rest of the night Taray behaved as if she did not exist, as if their exchange of glances had been nothing but a flicker of incense or a trick played on Fatma by her own eyes.

Covered by clouds of incense, creatures emerged from the sand to take part in the ostrich and camel races. Several of these strange travelers won valuable prizes offered by the Sheik, but when dawn arrived they abandoned their winnings and slipped away. The men of the tribe took the appearance and disappearance of shadow-knights and other creatures as a matter of course. From nowhere they came, into nothingness they vanished—this was their way. They traveled light and were indifferent to earthly rewards.

Sajir was sitting in a daze, with a look of permanent surprise on his face. "They lend a little heat and magic to our races," one of the warriors explained to him. "They ride in on horses sired by invisible stallions. It's just their way of lifting our spirits, that's all."

At that very moment Prince Taray was making his way over to Fatma.

"Why are you wearing a disguise?" he whispered.

She shivered. The smoothness of his voice made her think of a snake's new skin.

"Was it just curiosity," Taray asked, "that brought such a rare bird as yourself to our rude gathering?"

Then he went over to Sajir and told him the story of his life, speaking of himself in the third person as "the newcomer."

"He's a loner. When he was very young he fell in love with a desert nymph who visited him in dreams. He's forty-seven now, married and divorced twenty times, and still looking for the nymph. Every year he marries a new woman, because he believes that love can change any woman into a nymph. In the beginning, he wanted to be with the nymph before he bedded down with a human being. Now he's one of those men who keeps fooling himself, wasting his life on a mirage."

◆　◆　◆

The sun peeked from behind an immense dune on the horizon. Fatma felt the urge to go and see what the sun was doing behind the dune. She climbed the rising sand, sinking to her calves, the soft grit sifting between her ankles and toes, a fresh breeze blowing in her face, intoxicating her.

He jumped on her back, flattening her, mounting her as he would a young mare. Her long black braids came undone as she struggled, pooling darkly on the sand.

Taray clamped his thighs around her. With one hand he bound her hands behind her back, with the other he caressed her braids. This was Fatma's first true physical contact with anyone. Both of them were panting.

"Some of the men in our tribe have braids as long as this," Taray said, "but not so fine, not so beautifully combed and scented and cared for. Like a baby . . ." He seemed to stagger as he sniffed the braids.

Fatma struggled, he tightened his legs. Her blood surged again. Her shaking made him breathe harder.

"This body belongs to no man," he whispered in her ear. "Can you feel your own body under me? This mound of softness? Like a serpent or a sand-nymph! It's so alive, it feels like spears shooting through me. Here, touch yourself."

He placed one of her hands on her buttock. When she resisted, he let go. Her hand slipped into the sand and lay still. She looked at the red sand her hand was lying on. She saw red blood in her veins.

"I could rip your clothes off right now," Taray said, "and see you as you really are. But I hold you in respect. Not because you're a guest of the Prince — it's your choice I respect. You have to come to me of your own free will. You are the one who must come to me and tear off your clothes and show me what a woman you are. Then the whole desert would respect our choice, our union, our knowledge of one another."

He rolled away and sat up watching her.

In one breathless motion she jumped to her feet, rearranged her hair, and backed away. She felt she'd been bitten by some kind of snake, attacked by an enemy or tyrant whose power she couldn't match, not yet. She wanted none of this until she'd had time to gather her wits and her strength.

◆　◆　◆

It was not the man, Taray, who brought Fatma's dead embers to life. It was Fatma's own body, her own touching of it. Her touch triggered the need to be touched. It seemed to come from nowhere, all at once, wild and free, this opening of a long-blocked sensitivity inside her, the springing-to-life of the feel and smell and taste of human skin.

She wanted the touch, she wanted to perfect many different touches; she wanted to know the rhythms of touch, hear its soaring, deafening tempos; wanted to feel the touching ebb away. She wanted to cling to the mane of touch, to ride it and sink back. She wanted to tap the mysteries in her soul that had been ruined by her father's detachment and her husband's cruelty.

It was not sexual contact she was thinking of, it was human intimacy, the closeness of similar souls. The language was physical, but she had yet to utter a word of it. She wanted her body to stutter on its alphabet, its storming instincts.

♦   ♦   ♦

That night a dream summoned her to a sandy court where an emerald cave stood waiting. A masked sentry escorted her inside. She roamed through a forest of emerald branches. Underfoot, beneath the transparent stones on the floor of the cave, she could see desert animals racing back and forth—red and white camels, jackals, lions, ostriches, deer, along with vicious scorpions, serpents, small dragons, shy moles, three-legged fish, and several octopuses. The snakes looked up at her reassuringly.

She came near a clump of lovely tall fig trees bent over a green pond. The branches were dripping sap into the water.

Taray sat in the middle of the pond watching her approach. A crowd of masked courtesans milled about, showing only their fiery black eyes. They washed Fatma's hands with amber still warm from the belly of a freshly slaughtered whale, then let her move on. As she came to the edge of the pond, Prince Taray rose from his fig-milk bath and knelt down facing her. With separate sighs, the spirits of the creatures living in the cave warmed the air and backed away from the pond.

The amber dribbling down Fatma's wrists told her what to do:

swiftly, lightly, she dipped her thumbs in the fig-milk and drew a circle on Taray's heart. Her hands fluttered down to the surface of the pond again. She raised her palms to his face and began bathing him with her fingertips. Her touch was more than a lover's touch; it was as if she were molding him in clay or bringing his shape out of stone. She was a worshipful sculptor—shaping his nose, his eyelids, his forehead, his jaw-line, his lips. She cupped his ears in her palms. Her little fingers entered his ears, probing and shaping the passageways, then slipped out, slowly, leaving his ear-chambers ringing with her touch. Prince Taray moaned, eyes closed.

With the heels of her hands she sculpted the column of his neck. She moved to his chest, rubbing it, then dropped down swiftly and stuck the little finger of her left hand lightly in his navel; then further down, gently probing every fold, muscle and shadow, stroking his buttocks, making a fist and slipping it between his legs, rubbing her knuckles against the backs of his knees, where she let her hands rest for awhile, vibrating against his resistance, until her fingers slipped on the fig-milk covering his calves and swept back up, higher again, molding and massaging his long sleek legs, stroking up and down, down to the soles of his feet, between each toe. She thought about his eyes and his eyelids, but decided to leave them alone, preferring to leave her sculpture eyeless.

She sat up and traced circles on his palms, then pressed her fingertips against his fingertips, flattening her palms against his, imprinting her love, her mind and her life on his flesh, breathing her desire into the fig-milk, willing the imprint to endure and be vivid.

"Two fates . . ." she whispered, ". . . identical."

The milk was soft. As it dried, it left a transparent mask on Prince Taray's skin. He rose to his feet like an idol made of pearl.

He wants not to be touched, Fatma thought, not at all sure what to think after truly touching another human being for the first time, knowing only that she was taking her first steps down a long and treacherous road. Her instincts led the way, guiding her hands, giving her fingers the power to discover life, and give it. She thought: *This is like giving life to a child, shaping its body inch by inch.*

All the while she was bathing the Prince, a dark green cloud floated underneath the pond as if carrying it on a royal carriage. Taray's eyes remained shut, but Fatma could sense his alertness. Though no one had ever told her so, she knew that fig-milk was the best protection against poison. He was covered with it; there was no way into him. She felt obscurely betrayed.

His hand shot down and pulled her face to his.

"You're angry with me," he said, "aren't you?"

She was speechless. She struggled to reply, but she was too angry to understand the reason for her anger; it was a rage of the senses.

"You want to remain out of reach!" she heard herself say.

He laughed, and droplets of fig-milk showered from his body. His beauty took her breath away. He clasped her chin between his thumb and forefinger and turned her head toward the forest of fig trees. Fatma was startled to see that the forest was a great snake, and the trees were branches of its enormous body. The snake was dripping venom into the pond.

"The sap from the trees is your sap," Taray whispered, his lips brushing her left shoulder blade. "And I have arranged this forest so that I can drown in it."

His whisper sent a shudder down to her toes. She felt relieved.

◆　◆　◆

When she woke up, the Book of Dreams lay waiting for her, open to the chapter on figs and poison. When she touched the words, the image of what was written took shape in her heart:

The fig signifies a flood of abundance, in money and offspring. The Prince of the Yami is destined to reach the height of fame. It is written that he must be reborn, and soon.

Fatma contemplated the symbols of rebirth she had seen—the pond, the animals, the dense cloud scudding under the pond while she bathed the Prince. There were so many animals, and the vital ones—the dragons, lions, and fish—overpowered the creatures symbolizing envy: the jackals, scorpions, and camels. The racing cloud bolstered the positive signs, leaving no chance for a bad outcome. As for Fatma's sense of betrayal, that seemed to have something to do with the cave itself, the entrance to her dream.

She flipped the pages looking for the book's interpretation of poison.

Poison signifies treasure. The more serious the poisonous wound, the greater is the treasure to be won. Whoever drinks from the springs of poison is sure to be set free from whatever is imprisoning him. At the very least, he will marry an enchanting nymph.

Fatma closed the book. The scent of fresh fig-milk rose from the pages, shrouding her as she trembled.

◆   ◆   ◆

Three nights later, shortly after she had fallen asleep over her needle and thread, the old poet Ibn Madhy approached her truck. She woke to the rattling of the tailgate and the rumble of a deep voice.

"Open the cage, Little Nurse! I've come to take you away!"

Fatma put on her mask and white turban and jumped out of the truck. The poet-storyteller glared at her.

"I would have thought you'd have a better disguise," he said. "Don't be surprised, granddaughter of the Queen of Long Life; I saw you coming long before you were born. I was in love with your grandmother. I've dreamed about you coming in disguise to this desert garden of Najran, to the kingdom of reptiles. I even wrote some poems about your appearance in King Nasra's court."

Fatma was not at all surprised. She had dreamed about him when she was ten years old, this immortal man who had watched her so intently while her flag holder stood by watching the two of them, the girl and the old poet, play out their fates.

"All right," Ibn Madhy said tenderly, "so you're not surprised. But at least you should ask how old I am."

"You come from the tribe that discovered the spring of al-Khidr," Fatma said. She realized that these words, which came to her lips spontaneously, were her grandmother's rather than her own.

They set off a wicked quiver in the old man. "So you're a believer in the invisible springs?" he said, laughing. "The ones that exist only inside our rib cages? I thought I was the only one who believed in them. Well then, let me tell you what else I believe—they are nothing compared to the spring that was your grandmother. I've spent my whole life looking for comfort in women's arms. And yes, I found the spring—once—and I lapped its green milk like a man dying of thirst."

"What brought you here?" Fatma asked. "What are you doing among the Yami? Why have you come all the way from the land of the T'meem?" She was anxious to hear any news of her grandmother, who was of the T'meem tribe in the middle-north.

The old poet searched her face and hesitated for a moment before remembering the purpose of his visit. He renewed his decision to confide in her.

"According to the prophecy of Lar," he said, "you are a descendent of the Feathered Green One. As you probably know, he will come soon, and suddenly, to the kingdom of Najran, in the northeast. I am one of his soldiers. My mission is to pay homage to the granddaughter of our leader. I've also come because I was curious to sniff your scent up close. There's only one thing that's kept me alive all these years, and that's the scent of a real woman. So good night then, and have a safe trip, you and your temperamental companions."

He left Fatma sitting in amazement, uncertain whether he had actually knocked on the door of her cage or whether he was just a figment of her imagination.

Noor studied her reaction thoughtfully. Hearing nothing from her, he wriggled on the black silk of the *abaya*, turning the pages of the Book of Old Najran.

Fatma turned silently toward the book and entered it. Noor escorted her to a grand and ancient kingdom where she wore green silk and was human no more. Nothing remained of her former shape but the larva of fierce black fire crawling up and down her spine. The fire was enclosed in a warm transparent skin of blazing gold feathers.

She passed through the colonnades of the court as a glowing emerald serpent and approached the throne. A huge snake came forward to greet her, then slithered past her. Fatma felt a great warmth entering her, charging her center.

She found herself in the company of the king, who was introducing her to his subjects. Their images were contained in an enormous jewel. Looking closely at the gem, she recognized the prisoners of the snake farm, all the serpents who had stood by her during her years of marriage. Each snake wore a crown, and all of them were rearing their heads over enormous mounds of treasures. They gazed back at Fatma with kind, knowing eyes, understanding and appreciating her talent for traveling in the rich inner worlds they were so fond of.

She was dazzled. Everything in the courtyard gleamed with energy, displaying secret sources of power and loveliness. The king was ensconced on a tower of pure onyx. Reflections of the tower's blackness echoed in the deep violet rings on his body; purple storm clouds circled the tower.

Standing in a drizzle of pure musk, Fatma felt drunk with it all. Suddenly, as her eyes wandered over the grassy fields, she was able to see through things, through the white mountains and trees, the white earth, through time itself. Without saying a word, simply by showing her these wonders, the king was saying: *Whoever looks, really looks, into the essence of the inner world will see his own reflection. We are the creators of our own heavens and hells. And you are a queen.*

Fatma looked again and saw her own image running in the river that coursed through the flesh and bones of the world. Everything in the world was being carried along by the river. Deep in her veins she felt the roar of the river and the flood of creatures and elements within it.

She was no longer standing by the onyx tower in the courtyard. She was out there, somewhere, running everywhere at once, up and down like wind-tossed rain, scattering, splattering, soaring. She was carrying the kingdom and its king and all the courtesans of Najran in her blood. Her blood was white now.

Now it was purple. Then it was clear, transparent, reflecting every flicker of light, every thud of silence.

7   *Her Body Rebels*

y husband is a very tidy man. He eats beautifully—never a crumb on those beautiful lips of his. But he's neatest of all when it comes to my body. He positions himself between my wide-open legs without touching my skin at all. His sword flashes inside me without touching my walls or secret chambers. He reaches my inner door and knocks down the room at the center of me. Then he pulls back, quickly."

Relaxed by the sun and the sand, Fatma had gotten into the habit of revealing all her thoughts to Noor. She needed more of the dark understanding she had experienced while sitting by the stone wash basin.

"I've developed a certain skill," she went on, "the ability to float away while he's knocking against my forgotten center. I don't feel him anymore."

Traveling with the snakes had one great advantage: Sajir left her alone. He stuck to his plan of disguising her as a boy, and apparently came to think of her as one. He also seemed to have put aside his anger and determination to destroy her, body and soul.

The truck driver stayed with them and Sajir stayed with the driver, leaving Fatma to her reptiles. It may have been that he was frightened of intruding on her bed while it was surrounded by the snakes. Whatever the reason, for more than a month she was left to herself to heal.

♦   ♦   ♦

One night she left the Sheik's quarters to do some cleaning up. The snake truck was parked near a palm grove next to a lake formed by recent rains. As Fatma was walking by the edge of the water, a hand shot out from behind the palm fronds. It happened too quickly for her even to gasp—she was snared by strong black arms and pulled flat against her attacker's chest. Her body knew his at once, but terror muddled her instincts, and all she could do was struggle wildly to escape.

He said nothing, only chuckled, letting her spend her rage. When in the peak of her fury she pushed against him, he lowered his mouth on hers. Her lips trembled; she was paralyzed. Her will to fight ebbed and she began to lose track of time. He tantalized her by brushing his lips against hers without touching her mask or nipping her. The pressure of their mouths sent bolts of fire through both of them. She freed one of her hands and slapped him hard. He staggered and held on tight. Fatma felt dazed by her own savagery, swept away on a surge of fury.

In the silence that followed, she could feel the snakes moving blindly in the distance, then crawling across Taray's chest and hers and slinking up the hot path of her backbone. She swayed. The snakes watched. Their spirits were entering Taray, goading him to take her.

His whisper walked on her spine. "In the desert, love is honored. All you have to say is yes, and everyone will bless our union."

She flopped her head from side to side, unintentionally scuffing his lips again. She gasped when he yanked the mask away. He glared at the tattoo running down from her chin and tickled it with the tip of his tongue.

"You'll get poisoned!" she said, nearly choking on her words.

He staggered backwards, staring in disbelief. "This . . ." he said hoarsely, ". . . this is the first time I've heard you say a single word. But you're not really saying words, you're doing something else—chirping, or something not human. I couldn't understand what you just said, not the actual words, if I thought I was listening to human language. But the sounds you just made are the sounds I *should* be hearing from you. You're a desert nymph and you speak the language of nymphs. It's the sweetest sound in the world—the sound of a snake rustling through tall grass." He looked her in the eye and whispered fiercely: "Breathe again!"

"You'll get poisoned," she repeated softly.

Indeed, the sound she made was not human. This was the first time she had truly conversed with anyone from the outside world, and she discovered that the language she used was other than human; it seemed a mixture of wind and the slithering of snakes.

Taray understood her. He tensed and strained forward, as if sipping blueness from the air between them. "You've already poisoned . . ." he began.

She leaned away from his touch. He let her go. Her movement exposed more of the tattoo on her neck and below. His eyes tracked it down her body. She shivered easily out of his arms and backed further away. He kept looking at the tattoo, trying to touch her at a distance, just as he'd tried to touch her when he'd held her in his arms. Fatma sensed he was crumpling with loss—his loss or hers, she couldn't be sure.

"I'd love to run my fingers along that tattoo," he said. "It's more like a birthmark, really. I dreamed I had a tattoo just like it once, running all the way down from my chin to my navel. I was a lost soul in those days, truly. I walked the desert, getting lost in the dunes, throwing away everything I owned—rifle, dagger, horse, clothes. I passed out under a ledge of salt rocks and from a rock high above me, a sort of blueness started trickling down. The rock sent a serpent of water splashing over my chest, and on this river-snake nymphs of the desert were floating. The way they moved . . . their gestures pulled me back from the brink; they saved me.

"Since then no thirst has bothered me. Except my thirst for you. You're not a woman, you're not a man. You are a nymph, a queen of nymphs. Your poison crept into the vault where I keep my first and greatest loss locked away. I've been wandering ever since. Now I'm dying—did you know that? I'm standing here still feeling you in my ribs, in my legs. You're a river, your blue waters are dripping on my tongue. Why don't we go to the Sheik now and tell him I've become one of your victims. Why keep this crime—this victory of yours—a secret?"

"Love is not a crime, as you pointed out." Fatma laughed. She was a charming tease.

He slipped a silver dagger from his holster. "It is the nymphs' habit to kill errant knights, isn't it? I understand it's their greatest pleasure."

He flashed the dagger along her tattoo. Then he knelt down and drew mysterious symbols in the rich soil at the base of a palm tree.

"I could inscribe an amulet here," he said, looking up suddenly, "a spell that would tie you to me forever. Then I'd have the deadliest seeress in the desert under my control. So what do you think—do you want to come to me because of magic? Or love?"

He looked at her for a long time, as long as it took him to think better of his scheme.

"No," he said finally. "I want you to cross the secret barrier yourself; I want you to master your fears and frozen passions. I rather like the idea of waiting for you to cross the line. I want the storms, the saltiness, the tall grass, the tiniest gems—I want all of you."

He waited for her to say something. "Nothing I say gets your sympathy, does it?" he sighed. His eyes turned hard as they swept over her. "Can't I even make you feel sorry for me?"

"For *you?*"

"If feeling sorry for me would tempt you into my cave and bring you within reach of my claws, then I'd like nothing better than to fill you with sorrow. Don't you believe me, my little snake-shepherdess?"

The genuine distress beneath Taray's banter gripped Fatma by the throat. She was unable to breathe, much less speak. She stood there suffocated by his dark mood, waiting for someone to rescue her, for a falcon to swoop down and snatch her away to some unreachable mountaintop where she could forget the few things she'd learned about human contact.

What did she know? She knew now that she had a body, and she wondered if people noticed the difference in her. She had substance—she wanted everyone to see that. She wanted eyes to look inside her, wanted arms to circle her waist. She had a spine on fire, and she had lips too. Yes, most of all, she had lips—masked lips, but lips all the same. And a birthmark, or at least Taray thought so. Not just a complicated tattoo—a birthmark, a sign of her naked, natural self!

It occurred to Fatma that the birthmark might hold the meaning of her life: born of a snake's passion, she lived among the snakes like a child they needed to shelter from some fatal passion. Maybe the snakes fought against the eruption of her passion because they were afraid it would poison them and make them grow old.

She let the coldness she had lived with all her life wash over her. She accepted it as she accepted her blank-eyed friends.

◆   ◆   ◆

The old poet Ibn Madhy came to visit her again.

"You've been introduced to this valley's history of whiteness," he said. "Now it's time for you to see its history of water."

Fatma and the poet set off in the middle of the night and walked beyond the perimeter of the city, heading south. As they approached the foothills of a vast mountain chain, she gazed upon the most astonishing stones and boulders she'd ever seen. They were so huge that their peaks reached to the Seventh Heaven. Some of the stones were shaped like the hearts of enormous oysters, their black-brown shells cracked open and their yellow rock-meat throbbing toward the stars. Strewn like a giant's discarded belt around the foot of the mountains, the stones gleamed gemlike, ready to burst and drizzle the juice of their souls on the sand. Fatma realized they must be the ruins of an ancient dam.

"This is the Queen of Sheba's dam," Ibn Madhy confirmed. "There was a time when these stones lived a life of unparalleled richness. Each one held within itself a great flood. Since water is the sap of life, it's important to know the story of these particular stones. If you look closely you might see images hidden in their thick, silent skins. You might hear echoes of remarkable creatures, and read signs of the countless civilizations that flourished during the great Queen's reign."

On the oyster-flesh of one of the rocks Fatma noticed a troop of ancient warriors etched with a knife. The warriors were in mid-battle, fighting on horseback, hurling spears in long arcs, frozen in mid-

thrust. One of them, the highest-ranking knight, stood apart from the others, radiant on his huge stallion. To Fatma's surprise, he looked straight at her. She felt his spear flying through her heart, and she caught her breath. Ibn Madhy looked around to see what was bothering her, but saw nothing. The knight remained motionless on the stone, staring at Fatma.

The features of his golden face seemed familiar, intimately so, but she was so stunned that she could not place him or remember his name. She spent the rest of the night standing under the knight's poised spear, gazing at the miraculous stones. He vanished at dawn, along with his troop of warriors, disappearing deep into his rocky kingdom.

When the soldiers left, the stones, so dense and rough at night, became transparent and revealed hidden mirrors which seemed, by means of strange letters, to show time in reverse. The writing was vivid, alive; the script pulsed like the most exquisite snakes, swelling the rocks like flooding streams and coiling in circles that somehow completed the links between present, past, and future.

Fatma felt trapped in cycles of never-ending life, falling into them. She became a tunnel through which the energy of the universe flowed and the tunnel became a flute and the flute began singing magical, intoxicating music. Whatever the music touched turned to light, and everything that was solid flew off into space. She was in a world of light and the light was growing lighter. The energy, the light, and the music was a language. The language comprised the keys to the universe and Fatma was that language.

Ibn Madhy woke her up just before the first shaft of sun blinked over the mountaintops. On the way back to the truck, as they passed a shepherd milking his red-brown camels, the poet bought her a pot of thick milk. When she drank it she felt like a newborn taking her first suck from the nipple. This flavor, she knew, would stay on her tongue and in her memory forever. As she savored the plain, rich taste, it came to her that the face of the warrior on the stone was the same as her pursuer's; the ancient knight was none other than Prince Taray.

◆   ◆   ◆

The Yami understood that the older of their guests was a married man and the younger one was at liberty. Every Yami girl did her best to please the young man in the mask and capture him. This was the way the Yami went about things: the women snared men to expand their circle of life. So it was that Balkees, the most beautiful young woman of the tribe, set her heart on Fatma.

One evening Balkees came to Fatma's truck and lifted the curtain covering the back. Fatma was standing in the middle of the snakes sweeping the cage.

"Hello, snake shepherd!" Balkees called out. "I've brought you some honey from the mountain bees." She hesitated, shocked by the snakes—some of them were in the midst of an intimate moment. For a second Balkees forgot all about the snake shepherd she was visiting.

"We have a saying," she said at last, "that a woman's poison is more powerful than a snake's. Are you as clever with women as you are with your snakes?"

"I'm poisoned already," Fatma said, forced to respond to Balkees' teasing. "There isn't much more a woman could do to me."

"You don't sound like a man," Balkees said. "Men are usually afraid of women, or at least they pretend to be." Her dark eyes flashed all over the truck. She was more curious about the vehicle and its contents than she was about Fatma.

"You, on the other hand, are behaving just like a woman," Fatma said, having decided that attack was the best form of defense. "Prying

into things, playing up to the villagers' curiosity—isn't that what you're doing?"

Balkees threw the boy a haughty look and burst out laughing. Fatma laughed too, and their laughter showered the snakes like warm rain. Balkees' laughter was famous for bewitching any man within hearing distance.

She fell silent and watched Fatma groom the serpents' beds. Her mouth hung open as if sensing the currents and energy-paths Fatma was clearing. She opened herself to the waves emanating from the snake beds.

When Fatma finished her chores, the honey-girl came down to earth again. She glanced at the *abaya* hanging on the side of the truck and smiled. Smiling mischievously behind her veil, and doing it conspicuously, was an art Balkees had brought to perfection.

"A man who likes embroidery—ridiculous! That's a good joke for me, typical female that I am, to spread around the village, don't you think?" Balkees laughed. "Maybe we could make a deal, snake shepherd. Why don't you give me that *abaya* and I'll give you something to remember me by. Or would your woman be jealous? It *is* your lover's *abaya*, isn't it?" Balkees was genuinely curious.

Fatma could read the visitor's amorous intentions and wanted nothing to do with her. "Yes, it is," she said, desperate to find a shield.

"I could cast a spell of eternal love for you, snake shepherd. Would you let a peasant girl do something like that for you?" Balkees raised her hand imperiously, dictating obedience. Fatma had no choice but to hand over the *abaya*.

Balkees smiled contentedly, took a seat on a nearby rock, pulled out her supply of colorful twine, and proceeded to add some stitches. By the time she was finished, she'd added three red woolen triangles to the hood of the *abaya*, each with a silver circle in its center, and at the very center of these centers was a sparkling spiral of gold.

"I spent ten years embroidering my wedding dress," Balkees announced. "So I know all the spells and what they can lead to."

The simple humanity of her statement touched Fatma deeply. She blinked at the first exchange of feeling she'd felt in the village. Her eyes were brimming.

"Crying is not something a man would do," Balkees whispered, staring. "No, not at all."

Fatma's eyes welled with unshed tears. She stood for what seemed forever watching Balkees walk gracefully away, the folds of her robe displaying a bit of silver as she swayed. She'd left a large pot of honey on the rock where she'd been sitting. It was the first real gift Fatma had ever received.

She was baffled. What was it about this trip to Najran? Everything was conspiring to open up some new need in her. Everything was forcing her to feel, feel, feel.

Balkees' gift of honey reminded her of the burning need she'd felt in Taray. Only last night she'd dreamed Taray was with her. With his left hand he'd touched the top of her turban and slowly unraveled it, turn by turn by turn by turn, until at last her crown of braids was uncovered. With his right hand he held the braids and unraveled them too, loosing strand after strand, letting them tumble from the crown. He grabbed the longest one, cut it off with a swift slice of his dagger, ripped open his shirt, and tied the braid around his bare waist. He shook as if struck by lightning.

Fatma woke up feeling restless. Taray and his electrifying belt were gone. She needed to go somewhere, anywhere.

She climbed out of the truck, made her way to the lake, and

waded into the water. She stood listening to the birds rustling high in the palms. Cool wetness lapped the tops of her thighs. The palms were heavy with huge bunches of dates. Black birds nestled among them pecking at their sweetness and sipping the silence of dawn.

Fatma thought about her pursuer. Taray knew she was going to leave soon and he was furious with her, following her everywhere, hardly ever leaving her alone. If he kept it up, her true identity was bound to be revealed.

She was gazing at her reflection in the water when he appeared beside her.

"I could carry you off right now and disappear into the desert," he announced without ceremony. "I could hold you captive in one of the salt caves; no one would find us. If you know the desert, you know that no one would dare follow us. It's too wild, too treacherous, and no human being has ever set eyes on the salt caves. They are green, the caves; in the desert they bloom like ripe emeralds. And the only way to be in the salt caves is to be naked."

He paused to let this rule sink in. There was no need, because to Fatma it made instinctive sense.

"I can see you there on a full-moon night," he continued, "stretched out as smooth as a snake while the moonlight filters through the walls—the walls have suddenly become transparent, of course—and the moonlight splashes like a rainbow across your skin.

"No one but I has ever seen anything so beautiful. The first time I set foot in the caves I saw a vision of you—only a vision, but unmistakably you. You may think of yourself as my queen or my captive, whichever suits you. But remember, there isn't a prince or a knight alive who could stop me once I decide to take you.

"So picture yourself in a salt cave with your snakes lazing around you; picture yourself in this place where no rules apply, no bonds can hold you. And listen when I say that you must surrender to my desire. *You are mine.* I found you where no one else thought to look, in a cage full of snakes, dressed in ragged clothes like an ordinary boy. The law of the desert is clear: whoever finds a drop of water, it belongs to him. You've never been claimed; you're mine."

"I'm married," she said.

Her words jabbed him. He looked at her incredulously and laughed. "Who do you think you're fooling? No one has ever laid a hand on you."

"I am married."

He still did not believe her. "I know the Untouched when I see it. You are untouched. Go ahead and invent a husband for yourself if you like. It's just a technicality, simple to fix. Marriage is not a life sentence. I can see to it that your status is changed; rules are made to be played with. It doesn't make sense to mate a fine mare with a eunuch. That's the way our law works in these parts, and people respect it. In all the forty villages of our tribe, you won't find a single woman living with a man against her will. Some women may hate the men they live with, but if they do, they hate them of their own free will."

"There is one woman I know," Fatma said, "who is serving a life sentence."

Taray was incensed by the matter-of-factness with which she pronounced her own fate. "You *are* poison," he said. "You shouldn't be bathing in this lake, you'll kill the palm trees on the shore."

He turned to leave, snagging his sleeve on a palm frond. As he walked away, Fatma caught a glimpse of the dark braid circling his waist. With dreamlike slowness, she raised her hand and fingered the bristles in the spot where her braid had been cut. She nearly doubled over with longing. Back in the truck, the snakes stirred, sprinkled by the mist of passion showering from their mistress.

Fatma stood in the lake sensing the currents of the three rivers that ran into the narrow valley of Najran, gathering life from many, many directions. This was truly a land of plenty, and if she managed to live the life of wide horizons she wanted so much to live, she would love to return here one day, to this place of refuge.

The rivers answered her longing, roaring down the mountains that shielded Najran on the south and west. The prayers of ancient pilgrims echoed on the peak of Taslal, where the ruins of Najran's own al-Ka'aba, the sacred stone, were shining. The gleaming temple was a replica of the holy mosque in Mecca; it had been built in a foolish attempt to focus the heart of the world on the little valley and attract pious travelers to Najran.

◆   ◆   ◆

The rivers ran faster, foaming. The people of the village were cheering. The roads were jammed with brightly robed men dancing *al-Zamel* in honor of their departing guests. Behind them stood row upon row of swordsmen and women, flowered headdresses bobbing.

The snake truck gathered speed. The dancers high-stepped after it, trailed by women in black, silver anklets jangling, and still more women in yellow gowns, others in flowered skirts—and behind them, swaying to the pounding of the drums, came the camels, silver-braided saddles jingling, echoing the bouncing braids of hundreds and hundreds of women.

From the back of the truck, in what seemed an endless reverie, Fatma watched the crowd of Najranis recede like a backward-flowing river rushing toward the holy city of Mecca, so far away.

Taray's parting words still rang in her ears. He was here, with her, in the black silk of her *abaya*.

◆　　◆　　◆

That was where they found him.

Immediately after the snake shepherd's departure, the whole tribe went looking for the prince. His riderless horse had called attention to his absence. For two days the horse stood tethered by the side of the lake. There was no sign of Taray, who had never been known to go anywhere without his priceless stallion.

When one of the tribesmen loosed the horse's reins, the animal stomped the dust, cantered out of the village, and set off down the road taken by the snake shepherd in the truck. A search party raced ahead to detain the departing guests. A brigade of soldiers blocked the road and inquired if anyone had seen the vanished knight.

Approaching the rear of the truck, Taray's stallion rolled its eyes, reared up and began frothing at the mouth. When the tribesmen lowered the tailgate they found Taray, crown prince of the Yami, tangled in the coils of an enormous snake. They struggled to free him but wherever they tugged at the snake, its body turned to liquid. At last, with a mighty pull, they yanked off its black skin and tossed it by the side of the road, where it settled in the dust like a discarded *abaya*. When they looked again at Taray, the snake was still lying with him like a devoted lover, only now it was a gold-green color, glowing, and running like water all over the prince's body. The tribesmen hacked and slashed at the green skin with their daggers.

No one inquired about Fatma, not even her husband, who was standing around in shock. The masked boy was nowhere to be seen — a fact not lost on the knights as they carried Taray to safety. The prince was babbling incoherently.

The leader of the search party took Sajir aside. "It's not your fault," he said, coughing (the air had become a cloud of green dust). "This is an illusion, more like a dust-snake than the real thing. We're doing battle with a mirage that shed its black skin for a green one. Look at this green dust, it's like grime on a painting. It's turned our lord Taray into a mad poet. He's possessed for all eternity, the way poets are."

The prince's fever was so high that his skin singed the hands of the men carrying him away. Only his horse could tolerate the invisible flames licking his master.

The Prince was carried back to the lake near the village, where the tribesmen, who believed in the power of water to quench invisible as well as visible fires, prepared a mud bath. They brought Taray to the very same spot where Fatma had bathed the night before and lowered him into the water, which had an odd, musky odor. His fever climbed higher. No one was able to get close to him, much less touch his body. He began calling out for a masked lover, or so it seemed to the tribesmen.

Rumors about this extraordinary display of passion swept through the village. "He deserted his nymph-lover," the old men muttered. "He stayed too long among ordinary mortals. Not even a knight can trifle with a woman from the invisible world. She crushed him."

They carried him off at last to the hunters' tent, where it was thought that his love of sandstorms might return and quench the inferno raging inside him. An old seeress was called in to treat him. For an entire month he lay unconscious, surrounded by a circle of silver daggers buried points-up in the sand. This treatment was prescribed by the seeress as the most effective antidote to poison with inflammable properties. At night the daggers picked up glints of moonlight and cast their beams in a silvery circle under the prince's bed. During the day the daggers reflected the desert sun, concentrating its rays and creating a mirage-bed to support his body, so that whatever the hour he seemed to be floating on a magical liquid. At midday, when the sun was most ferocious, the attendant knights saw steam hissing off the dagger-tips, confirming their belief that the blades were doing battle with the invisible fires of the hell inside their prince.

The women put on black garments in anticipation of his death. Twenty high-ranking maidens shepherded Taray's flock of thorough-bred white camels toward the great tent to have one last look at their master.

The seeress was curious to find out everything she could about the nymph or snake shepherdess who had infected Taray. The seeress thought she might have sighted her once, approaching the camp at twilight, walking out of the dusk and sitting down next to Taray's sick bed, entertaining him with poetry, caressing the verses with the sweet intensity of someone fondling gems. The verses overheard by the seeress were well-known and highly esteemed by the bards of Arabia.

The seeress owned an odd-looking she-camel. This camel was unique among the animals of the desert in that its body was bright red and its neck pitch-black. It was to this creature that the seeress was in the habit of confiding all her secrets.

"In the legendary valley of Ubbqar," she whispered to her ever-attentive dromedary, "there lives a nymph who hides in quicksand and mirages. This is the same nymph who spent a night with the prince and departed as soon as the sun was high enough to create the first mirage of the day."

"And they say she is descended from the extinct oryx," added one of the prince's shepherds, who made a point of keeping the seeress's strange camel at a safe distance from his herd of normal, white-brown beasts.

The seeress was determined to find out more about the masked boy who traveled with the collection of snakes. She probed the prince's entire body, even his fingernails and intimate orifices, and collected traces of Fatma's scent. He reeked of musk.

The seeress came to the conclusion that her patient had to be treated with fire. She arranged for him to laid down next to a heap of tamarisk branches and ordered his sandals removed. She passed a blazing stick over the sole of his right foot, then his left. He showed no signs of pain or reflexive feeling, but the prince's brother winced when he saw white streaks running up and down Taray's body, radiating from the spot where the seeress was treating him. When the white streaks came into contact with the fire itself, the scent of musk grew so strong that it filled the entire tent, and the streaks ignited like rivers of fire, splashing still more musk-fumes around.

"Now his body is free of musk-soldiers," the seeress announced with satisfaction. Then she turned to her she-camel and covered her mouth so no one could hear. "But I have my doubts," she whispered, "about his ever recovering from those poems about the green caves."

When the first crescent of the new moon appeared, the prince stood up and walked away from his bed. Those who witnessed his recovery were dumfounded. Taray looked at least twenty years younger than his forty-seven years—"as if reborn of the poison," people said.

Though the prince continued to recite poems of undying love, he took no further interest in women. It was said that he had come into his inheritance—meaning the treasure of his gem-verses—and that the poems that rolled off his tongue flowed to the very edge of the desert and beyond, into the realms of the wandering tribes. Not a single knight sallied forth into the desert without wrapping his arrows in copies of Taray's verse-gems. No lover failed to put his poetry to use in pursuit of nymphs, gazelles, and other objects of passionate desire.

As for Taray himself, he set out far into the wilderness, on a long journey down the road of solitude. Never again did anyone lay eyes on the Prince of the Yami.

♦ ♦ ♦

Fatma was silent as a stone all the way home; it was as if she were no longer present. Even Sajir sensed the ominous aura about her. More and more, she gave herself over to the snakes. Her body changed. She looked increasingly like a serpent—in the sleekness of her movements, the glow of her skin, and the cast of her eyes, which seemed to look inward at a secret world.

What frightened Sajir was the noiseless way she moved. "You can't hear her coming," he muttered. "It's like she's a shadow or a flickering light. Or an actual snake."

Every now and then she surprised him by popping up behind him when he thought she was asleep in the back of the truck. One night he peeked into the cage. He could barely distinguish her from the snakes. They were all coiled together in one great ball of skin; Fatma's skin was glowing green.

Sajir was anxious to get home as fast as possible. At home she would forget all this wildness and obey him once more.

♦ ♦ ♦

All during the trip home Fatma was deluged by torrential feelings and visions of bodies. Whenever she closed her eyes, even in the middle of the day, it was always the same dream.

She saw herself totally naked, made entirely of amber, racing over the desert's ancient trading routes in the days when amber was more precious than gold. She was being stalked by huntsmen, knights, and traders trying to capture her as a valuable piece of merchandise (her curves were carved of priceless incense).

Swiftly as dust borne on a bright wind, she ran toward Najran. She made her way to the lake ringed by sentry palms and tied herself to the trunk of a lone palm rising from the middle of the lake. Her pursuers joined the villagers in celebrating her arrival.

The surface of the lake was utterly still, glazed. Thousands of people milled on the shoreline, rank upon gaudy rank of them—the men in red and yellow, the women in silver and gold, the animals in green, purple, and black. They let out a great roar and began dancing the *al-Zamel* dance. The pounding violet drums sparked violet sparks.

The seeress stood at the head of the throng carrying a big branch from a tamarisk tree. The crowd of people and animals, swaying as if bewitched, followed the seeress as she walked across the water. The drums beat louder. The water splashed high up the women's hennaed ankles, but no one sank, not a single soul, and everyone arrived effortlessly at the palm tree where Fatma was tied.

When the seeress stepped forward, Taray materialized next to his lover, stark naked and swaying. His body was sculpted of solid emerald, or perhaps of stone from the salt caves.

When the seeress began lashing his back with her tamarisk branch, the branch burst into purple flames. Taray danced away and disappeared into the fire. The seeress blew on her stick, the purple flames flared viciously, and in one quick swoop she transferred the fire to Fatma, whose amber body ignited with a roar, flared up, and was swiftly reduced to fragrant, smoldering embers, blindingly bright. The sparks hissed in the water, which, to everyone's astonishment, turned into a thick silvery substance from which Fatma's body (or the magical incense-fumes her body now was) shot up, flaring again. The air was filled with the scent of amber, the dancers went wild, stomping and marching like an army gone mad, each soldier approaching Fatma's fire, scuffing his skin against hers, twirling around and dancing in circles around her. Every part of every dancer's body rubbed hungrily against her. Men, women and animals joined the ritual of circling the blazing mother-fire, and everyone snatched a flame for himself.

The camels and horses were especially striking in their violet-green sparks. Their graceful necks flowered with rings of fire; the horses' manes burst into flames and raced into the woman who had become an amber pyre. Fatma's hair swished across her eyes like a mare's mane. She tossed her head back and stretched her neck further and further, ever more gracefully, invitingly, until she seemed a creature very like a horse, a snake, a camel, and a gazelle all at the same time.

King Nasra himself set crowns on her head, on her soft shoulders, and on her upturned breasts, while thousands upon thousands of his courtiers longingly caressed her slim legs and the seductive bulge of her belly. Her blue birthmark-tattoo trickled down her torso in a river of flashing blue fire. Whatever the fire touched turned at once to sapphire, then melted in the intense heat and became a mist of blue incense that condensed into blue beads spangling the shoulders, breasts, and brows of the dancers with a sparkle such as only the ancient gods were said to possess.

Then came the falcons—flapping around her, masks melting, eyes fierce and naked to the world, feathers catching fire as they soared high above the lines of dancers. The birds dipped their feathers in the lake of the sky and swooped down on Fatma, fanning the incense, showering the celebrants and intoxicating them with perfume.

Snakes and jackals joined the adoring dance, and all became one great whirling cloud of incense.

Fatma woke up feeling pregnant. She groaned as if about to go into labor.

◆   ◆   ◆

She tried hard to keep the dream going, and to remember the shock of Taray's leaving, but all she could remember was the old poet Ibn Madhy, standing in silence watching her work on her embroidery, as he had during that last night she'd spent in Najran. He looked so sad, staring at her like someone about to deliver a funeral oration. Fatma was unable to speak. She felt the familiar urge to vanish.

"What do your dreams have to say about my future?" she asked lightly, wanting to brighten his mood.

The old poet looked surprised. He handed her an amulet, a silver square exquisitely embossed with a tangle of snakes in the form of protective spells. Inscribed within the snakes were lines of poetry that Fatma could not quite make out.

"This is a precious relic from the world that used to be," Ibn Madhy said. "I came by this treasure one night when I wandered away from the prince's tent after a wonderful evening of poetry. Everyone was in a trance of ecstasy. The chief poet of the tribe proclaimed that I, Ibn Madhy, was possessed by the spirits of Ubbqar, that in fact I was singing their secret songs. But I wasn't in the mood to linger with mere mortals, so when everyone fell asleep I left the camp and went into the forbidden zone, far out into the dunes. I was in a fever—truly I was a poet possessed.

"I reached the horizon where dawn shatters the darkness as if shedding the blood of a deer so elusive it scarcely exists. I was stopped by a beautiful *houri*. When she whispered my name, the sweetness of her voice speared me to the spot. I looked up at her and saw that her body was made of fine, rose-colored sand. Her skin was aglow. She laid me down on sand of the very same rose color and chanted poems in my ear. The poems made me drunk, her voice rattled my heart and boiled the blood in my veins. The taste of her rosy roundness was sweet on my tongue. By the time she left I was completely drunk from drinking her in. Then I woke up. She was gone.

"She left behind this amulet, and the echo of her voice telling me where it had come from. Originally it was the key to king Nasra's secret vault, which was located in the center of the great stone dam. This dam did more than hold back the waters; it was also a repository for the chronicles of ancient kings and epics of chivalrous deeds. Over the course of time, the key dropped out of sight. But its heart was rescued and preserved by a tribe of geniis known as Banee al-Asfar. Here it is."

Ibn Madhy set the key down on Fatma's *abaya* and vanished into the night. She watched the key dissolve into the black silk, puddling in a pool of silver liquid or snake venom, spreading across the breast of the garment.

Chilled by what felt like a strange wind from the past, she slipped into the *abaya* and walked slowly through the midst of her blank-eyed subjects. She was beginning to feel rather ancient herself.

"You look like the great King Nasra," whispered Noor, eyeing her.

"A king?" she laughed. "A *man*-king?"

"This amulet contains thousands of servant-snakes," the shadow said. "Each one is finer than a strand of hair, and each one contains incredibly powerful poison and magic. Every single one of these creatures has enough force to destroy the mightiest enemy and enough power to keep you out of harm's way. You believe me, don't you?"

"I believe what I choose to believe," she said evenly.

"That's good. Because this magic works only for those who believe in it." Noor's tone turned grim. "Now listen closely to what I have to say. The key must remain in your *abaya*. It must never return to the door it came from. Keep this warning in mind if you have any interest in delaying your departure from this broken-legged world."

One after another, bolts of lightning lit up the dunes and boulders outside the truck. Just once, briefly, a flash of light entered the blackness where Fatma stood with her companions.

A few dunes away, shepherds noted the location of the lightning strikes and committed them to memory, intending to drive their herds to safe places that surely would not be struck again. Meanwhile, in the truck, the blank eyes of the snakes seemed to go truly blind when they saw the storm's most terrible bolt strike their shepherdess. But the snakes were not blind; they were watching the routes the lightning took as it crackled across her skin. They planned to travel these routes as soon as her body stopped smoldering.

◆   ◆   ◆

When Fatma returned home from her wild trip, she put the shadow back on the wall above the flint trough. She wiped her *abaya* against the stone, releasing Noor, who oozed back into the wall and took up his original position as naturally as if he'd never left it.

Sajir was shocked by the number of new species in the snake farm. The room was tightly sealed—no cracks in the walls, none on the floor or ceiling. The windows were firmly shut. Yet new snakes kept materializing, seeping into the room from out of nowhere, looking for Fatma's voice and warmth.

Sajir was knowledgeable enough about the snakes of Arabia to know that there were no more than forty species in the whole country and that they were concentrated in the southern and western areas, near the coast. Nevertheless, thousands of new species (or tribes, to use Fatma's word) were taking up residence in her reptilian kingdom. It was remarkable to see a specimen as fussy as the Wart Snake happily accepting whatever the woman served him.

Sajir found their show of mutual affection revolting. Privately he accused his wife of having sinful relationships with the snakes—either that or casting spells. It was the only possible explanation for her mastery of the vicious brutes. But business was flourishing, so he kept his suspicions to himself and never said a word to his snakewoman wife.

◆   ◆   ◆

Ramadan, the month of fasting, coincided with the arrival of the scorching wind called *al-Samoom*. Sajir's tongue was dry and cracked by the time the sun started to set, when the first drink of the day could be sipped and the first bite of food eaten. Fatma went about her business as usual, shrouded in the quiet rustling of her *abaya*, whose rivers of embroidery coursed all over her, trickling in and out of The Invisible. Her routine during the month of fasting was to spend the daylight hours with her snakes. Just before sunset she left them to prepare a meal for her husband, who invariably pretended to be sleeping. Her figure was becoming even more voluptuous and serpentlike; she moved as fluidly as the invisible rivers embroidered on her *abaya*.

Sajir, his rage mounting, took it all in. The mere sight of her in the dark silk gown stoked his anger and made him sweat profusely. Every time he looked in her direction, he felt a terrible pain in his chest. "The dark hell you're moving around in is spitting flames all over the room," he hissed.

Her hands moved to unfasten her *abaya*.

"Don't take it off!" he said, infuriated. "That hot hide of yours will suck the last bit of coolness out of the air. I can't stand it—I just can't!"

She knew he wanted her to go away, so she did, out into the streets of Mecca, where *al-Samoom* was spreading its madness. The hot wind lashed the cobblestones and nipped at people whose tempers had been rendered all the more irritable by their fasting.

◆   ◆   ◆

When Sajir stepped inside the snake farm after several months of staying away from it, he was blinded by the quality and color of the light. Sunlight was everywhere, filtered by colorful veils of sheer silk, meticulously arranged so they cast yellow light on snakes accustomed to living under desert sun, blue light on the nocturnal snakes, and green and brown light on snakes born in the rain forest. The room floated in the light like a bubble of pleasure and peace.

Sajir found this bubbliness intolerable; it made him feel beaten or somehow cheated out of something. He slammed the door and stalked out of the house. By the time he returned, he had refined his anger into a rage for revenge, tempered by stealth. In the middle of the night he peeked into the room and caught a glimpse of the strange lanterns that had been lit to enhance the glow coming from the tented veils. He couldn't be sure what sort of lanterns they were. They looked impossibly ancient, gossamer-like, unreal. If he didn't know better, he would have given in to his first impression, which was that they were incredibly huge precious stones. Whatever they were, the lanterns lent an undeniable air of intimacy and unreality to the bubble of colored light and shadow the snake farm had turned into. Sajir could not shake the conviction that the snake farm actually *was* a bubble, that the lanterns would vanish if he inquired about their origin, and that the merest sneeze or ill-timed look from him would shatter the whole farm. He knew he had trespassed on an utterly alien world.

His unease increased when he realized that Fatma was treating the snakes even more tenderly than before. Her skill and understanding were astounding. The bubble stayed at precisely the right temperature at all times, dropping a few degrees during the night. Fans fashioned from silk and straw kept the air fresh and moist, always within a degree or two of the optimal 80 degrees Fahrenheit.

How had his wife mastered these technical details? It had taken Sajir years to learn how to maintain constant temperature and keep it in the right range after sundown. Changing the temperature was an enormous undertaking with the crude instruments at his disposal. The average snake preferred daytime temperatures between 82 and 86 degrees. Desert snakes liked it higher — 86 to 90 degrees. During the night, it had to drop between 80 and 84. It was all a tremendous amount of trouble. If by any chance the temperature dropped near freezing or higher than 104, the results were fatal. More than once it occurred to Sajir to tinker with the controls so he could watch the snakes cook and sizzle and crackle — along with his witch of a wife.

His father had drilled the crucial importance of constant temperature into his son's brain. The poor old man used every trick he knew to impress on his son how essential it was to understand the snakes' sensitivity to change. Sajir pretended to believe what his father told him, but deep down he was resentful. He bridled at having to care about the needs of dumb creatures; it was a kind of enslavement, having to wait on blind masters and cater to their eccentric needs.

Nevertheless, the trip Fatma and Sajir had taken seemed to have increased her burning dedication to the snakes, and raised it to the unreasonable level of art.

◆   ◆   ◆

"Don't be shy, come closer." The shadow flickered, flamelike, as he spoke. "These comrades of yours were born in the fires of Arabia's ancient past. Actually, they are sparks from the ditch where Thonawas—the cursed king of old—incinerated the early martyrs to the faith. It happened in the distant past, more centuries ago than you have fingers and toes.

"The cruel king and his courtiers sat on their golden thrones watching the martyrs burn. King Thonawas supervised every detail of the executions. He spared no one—old people, children, animals, women—all were fuel for his great holocaust. Fans stirred acacia perfume to cover the stench of burning flesh. From the fires of the believers, the snakes sprouted. Sparks of burning flesh fell on the ground and turned into sleek, vengeful forms—this, by the way, is why most snakes live in the southwestern part of Arabia."

So spoke Noor. Fatma listened in fascination. The blue tattoo running from her lips to her navel ignited in sympathy with the blazing ditch where the martyrs had died. As it burned, the tattoo turned a lighter shade of blue, drawing life from the martyrs' boiling souls.

"Then the fire got out of control," the shadow continued. "It spread through the ranks of Thonawas's courtiers and soldiers, and soon the whole army was frantically clutching at the reins of the evil thing, the fire-serpent. At last they managed to bury it deep underground. The fire was commanded to stay there for all time, lest it sweep over the entire peninsula. Thonawas's power declined. Like a player leaving the stage, the famous king disappeared from the chronicles of Najran, and what once was his kingdom became the Kingdom of Snakes.

"Having started their lives as sparks, the serpent-sparks ignited certain stones. The stones arranged themselves into a castle, the grandest castle in the greatest kingdom in all Arabia. The evidence suggests that the Kingdom of Snakes flourished two millennia ago, when the southern part of Arabia was at the height of its power."

Noor pointed to a peculiar spot on the skin of the snakes in the farm. The spots, which were circled with a mosaic-like lines, appeared in different places on each snake. Some were nearly impossible to detect. "The snakes are very fond of this particular spot," Noor said. "It is a sort of brand, a precise image of the ancient Kingdom of Snakes, where all the snakes in the world come from. Come closer, come here. You can learn their secret language, it's the language spoken by your ancestors. Snakes are a hidden part of every human being, the fiery part that can eradicate pain and disease and overcome hell itself."

On the skin of every snake there appeared, as if reflected in a glass globe, a fence precisely 235 meters long by 220 meters wide; this represented the moat and the great city surrounding the castle of Najran. The fence was built of ordinary stones, large and small, irregularly shaped, pitted with protrusions and square depressions, arranged in checkerboard fashion and engraved with *musnad* signs, the ancient script used by the nomads of the south. The entire city was protected by towers and turreted castles, and its center was constructed of glazed ceramic. The city was intersected by two roads serving the traffic in perfumes, herbs, incense, and flax exported from the kingdoms of the south to the northern lands lying between two rivers. From there the road branched northwest toward the fertile crescent and the land of the Nile.

"Najran was and always will be the center of great wealth," said Noor, "and the envy of all the famous kings."

◆ ◆ ◆

Fatma's suspicion that she was pregnant grew stronger. She willed her body to display the seed hidden inside. She was filled with a desperate longing to bring into the world a new life, a human companion, nurtured by the trickling waters of her tattoo.

In an effort to stimulate the seed in her womb, she painted her belly with the most vivacious designs she could find on the snakes. Then, during the darkest hours of the darkest nights, she closed her eyes, covered them with black silk and journeyed toward the murky kingdom of her snakes. Completely blind, she groped along the zigzag routes on the snakes' bellies until she reached the realm where the serpents lived their invisible lives. There, on the outskirts of the kingdom, she came upon the Clown Snakes merrily lurking in carefree formations, ready as always to fill anyone who encountered them with profound delight. Fatma took in the freedom of their shapes and studied the ease of their movements. Around the triangle at the bottom of her belly she drew a border of joy.

She passed into the kingdom of the Wise Ones, the snakes whose skins bore symbols of the darkest secrets of the universe. As she came close to their mysterious patterns, she lost her own shape and became a drop of water shivering with expectation.

She realized that unless she penetrated to the heart of silence itself she would not be able to interpret the symbols on the Wise Snakes. She listened with all her might. The intensity of her listening exposed her long years of pain, and all her loneliness.

This silence taught her a new language, which in turn taught her the code of the other symbols. She stood face to face with the secret longing she'd lived with all her life. None of it had died, none of it was lost. Every breath she'd ever breathed, every spark of suffering and sensation, was there, pictured in simple, eloquent circles on the skins of the snakes. Their bodies were endless rivers running below the surface of the universe, eavesdropping on everything that was happening and everything that had happened, bearing the shadows of everything along on their currents. Nothing—not the tiniest twitch of a chrysalis, not one butterfly, not the slightest quiver of creation—was lost on the snakes; their mute sensitivity caught everything.

Fatma listened carefully. She could hear their calming essence. Their peacefulness pulsed in her womb. She wanted to make a bed of this calmness where her seed might spark to life, and breathe.

She woke up in the middle of the night. A streak of light appeared on her navel. There was no telling exactly what it was, though on close inspection it seemed about to turn into a whirlpool capable of blinding anyone who looked at it and sucking out his soul.

Sajir happened on her by accident while she was taking a shower. The sight took his breath away. He stared at her naked, tattooed body, and when he saw the light-streak on her navel, he began to choke as if drowning. Fatma continued standing in the shower, an empty pitcher raised over her head, looking past him at the shadow on the wall. The shadow was violet, the same color as the light on her belly. She concentrated on its flickering light; it looked like a seed, some kind of seed.

She looked down, saw that her belly was not swollen, and felt sad.

Sajir was disgusted by her snakey body and the snake-signs running like a dark blue river down from her chin to her nameless nowhere. At the source of the river, the spot of light glowed, a white pool shattering into a rainbow. Sajir quaked with feelings he could not name. He turned stiffly, a man whose passion for revenge was about to explode. He left the bathroom door ajar and disappeared into the crowded street.

Fatma stood in the silvery shower remembering last night's adventure and her reentry into the kingdom of Najran. She mounted her throne atop the castle's westernmost column and recalled the throngs of courtiers, the reptiles' fascinating formations, the clowns circling her, the magicians' nestling amid illusions, the bells jingling on the musicians' shirttails, the Master of Dyes splashing rainbows on the courtiers' faces and clothes, the hypnotist dancing in circles, mesmerizing the courtiers hungry to see into the heart of his spinning. The snakes twirled by the hypnotist were rare specimens. Everyone who looked at them immediately fell into a stupor, except for the high king of old Najran, who remained invisible behind his mask, listening to the confessions spilling from the lips of those who were hypnotized.

Actually, most of the snakes were wizards in disguise and kings from the realm of the geniis. They were escorted by row upon row of lovely serpents marching in rings around them. At the center of the wide circle stood courtiers adorned in plain, solid colors—blue, green, or silver. People who looked at them found their vision blurred at first, then sharpened when they caught sight of the supreme ruler of all snake-kings, the great-grandfather of Nasra, the most powerful monarch in the vision that was the land of Najran. This invisible grandsire, this awe-inspiring seer, was veiled by the subtlest sort of skin; a beautiful coat of labyrinths covered him completely. Courtiers circled him, waiting their turn to attend to the needs of the majestic shadow. And a shadow he truly was, for it was not fitting that the great grandsire should appear to them as flesh-and-blood, otherwise they would be turned into water or sand by the splendor of his magic. Each courtier reflected just a bit of the shadow, a hint of his design, a suggestion of movement, a seductive turn or sigh—image upon dazzling image, endlessly reflecting the infinite beauty, the unreachable essence, the veiled reality of their king.

Then, to the accompaniment of a melody whose loveliness was so refined that it surpassed absolute silence, the king bestowed his gifts. With the simplest, most profound kind of whisper, he summoned his courtiers to come closer and blend into his mask. With sudden, twisting steps, while the king-shadow itself twisted and turned, the chosen ones seeped into the shadow-king. Those left out could only gaze in wonder or squint at the mist of smoldering musk.

The chosen ones vanished. Kneeling, shrouded by the mask, they had turned the briefest of eye-blinks into symbols precisely inscribed on the king's body, sinking deeper every second, deeper and deeper into his real skin, his real soul, into the energy endlessly moving within.

It was the most amazing dance Fatma had ever seen. The shower water she was standing under took on an inky substance. In its shining ripples she could sense the courtiers' quick steps and the gracefulness of the spirit capturing them.

The shower room swelled, bursting with joy. The drops of water steamed away into bright scented vapor, drawing Fatma into their slow spiraling.

She had nearly turned to vapor herself when Sajir appeared at the front door calling her name, breaking the spell, and interrupting her trip. Returning to her body, she abandoned the reptiles' court till nightfall, when darkness would lead her within once more, back to their kingdom. Night was Fatma's time to roam the reptile kingdoms, to travel through vast shadowy realms, to reach the unreachable, to capture the uncaptured. She could still feel the snakes slithering inside herself, and she knew that her body and the masked king's were intimately acquainted.

Surely, she thought—surely now she was healed, surely she was safe from her husband's assaults. She relished her newfound sense of wholeness.

◆   ◆   ◆

The snake farm was in a pandemonium of propagation. Eggs of all colors lay everywhere, especially in the flint stone trough. Even the dusty old stones the house was built of began to change, becoming saturated with the heavy scent of female musk. Gradually the stones turned transparent and took on an enchanting emerald gleam—a wicked sort of shine, Sajir thought when he noticed it. The emerald glow spread tantalizingly along the floor between the snake farm and the bathroom. All this time, nestled in the flint trough, the eggs were going through a prolonged period of incubation, slowly turning transparent and displaying the dark dots of the new snakes' just-formed blind eyes. With an eery silence, the dots tracked the three colored triangles on the forehead of their queen and fed on the mysterious energy radiating from her body.

Fatma sat naked on the floor. Next to her lay her *abaya*, the night-black silk spread out like a river whose forbidden springs she wantonly sipped, her feelings overflowing their banks and pouring out of her. She was at once energized and peaceful.

The eggs took on the colors suggested by her emotions. As her feelings neared a climax, the eggs acquired the fiery essence of precious stones, diffusing a vivid glow of peace and contentment across the flint.

Fatma stopped working at her embroidery, assigning that task to the Sewing Serpents, an army of silver snakes who crisscrossed the silk in soldierly ranks leaving magical tracks of silvery saliva that dried into webs of exquisite stitches.

The whirlwind of her emotions, along with the relentlessly spreading emerald glow, drove Sajir further and further away. He felt harried, hunted down by the approaching threat of intimacy, revolted by it. He was sure it would devour him. And the growing aura of pregnancy that hovered soothingly around the house disgusted him.

"The place is poisoned," he muttered over and over.

♦ ♦ ♦

It was then that the dream started. For the first time since leaving Najran and her memories of it behind, Fatma saw the ancient stone knight again, riding in on his enormous stallion, assuming the role Ibn Madhy had played the night the old poet explained the water-history of Najran.

The knight led her once again up the southern mountains toward the dam. But this was different from her first visit: the boulders, once transparent, were guarded now by soldiers of stone, and displayed none of their inner treasures. There was an air of wariness and anxiety about the rocks, as if they feared the knight's intentions in guiding the kidnapped queen to their secrets for a second time. They hid their hearts in deep shade and lay in wait, expecting trouble.

Oblivious to their shadow-tricks, the knight ascended the dam, climbing its sleek rock face like the ghost of a goat with the wind at his back, leading Fatma higher and higher to a place where there was no light at all and no foothold, not even a crack where ghosts or winds could linger. He stopped, positioning himself between two crags that pointed up like arrow shafts. He pulled out a heavy, old-fashioned lance and began digging into the rock at the crest of the dark ridge, clawing savagely at the rock face, which yielded nothing but sparks (to Fatma they seemed arrows shot off in self-defense). He dodged the sparks and went on digging with the blind determination of a dreamer.

The rock face crumbled, exposing a colonnade leading to three arched doors buried under a layer of flint at the top of the dam. When Fatma and the knight came near, the doors fired off violet sparks to chase the intruders away. Fatma hid her face when she saw the sentry-statue standing over the doors, a three-headed warrior fashioned of black-veined flint. The stone guard was carrying an enormous spiky axe capable of crushing whatever came near. There he stood, eternally slashing the empty air.

The knight backed away, making room for Fatma to get a clear view of the doors. On top of each one she saw a sheet of gold studded with cruel-looking iron, and across the gold bands was an inscription inlaid with pure emerald:

A caged animal waits for its day of release. Nothing will stand against its evil energy. The writing continued in script of glittering rubies: *Hold your breath, say not a word, lest you stumble on the secret language and lock this charm away.*

The knight instructed Fatma to examine the writing inscribed on the door jambs. Endlessly it repeated: *These three doors of volcanic rock are not to be disturbed before the coming of the servant of the River Lar. When the time of the servant comes, these doors, sealed with words, will yield to the key he carries. He is allied with the geniis of Banee al-Asfar. Together they will bring about the fulfillment of the Peninsula's destiny.*

◆   ◆   ◆

Fatma's husband made a point of spending very little time in the house. Now and then he poked his face into the snake farm and harvested a bit of poison, but only as an excuse for going to the market, where he was not likely to be troubled by close contact with anyone.

Fatma moved among her wild pets dressed in a long, wide robe of gauze soaked with water from the vat. The snakes fed quietly, apparently on whiffs of her scent. When they sensed her passing their cages, they would stretch out and glide in lazy circles, savoring her warm glow, their blank eyes tracking her as she walked by.

She sat down at the flint trough. The shadow blinked at the wild freshness of her scent. The walls and bottom of the trough, she noticed, were covered with bright snake dust arranged in intersecting circles of green, dark blue, black, silver, red, and pale gold.

At Noor's suggestion, she slipped the gauzy robe from her shoulders, baring her silky breasts and belly. The robe lingered about her hips, with one or two folds falling to her knees. She looked down. As if of their own volition, her fingers found their way to the colored dust and knelt in it, one finger at a time, danced for a moment, then flew back up to her trembling body. Tenderly, with each finger, she drew circles on her belly, thousands of shining silvery circles. She was expecting a thunderbolt to strike her, pierce her womb, and fertilize her seed. She stood perfectly still watching the circles twine together, mating in a frenzy on her belly, while the dark blue river pulsed from her chin to the triangle between her thighs, dizzying every cell in her body. She was soaked in musky sweat.

She had fallen unconscious by the time the shadow left the wall and began inching closer, casting a dark shroud over her, cloaking her in a mysterious wildness that caused Noor's Book of Animals to appear. A world of strange creatures poured from its pages: falcons, wild golden camels, sand, and rocks on which messages were written, all of them circling Fatma, waking her up again in the whirl of their wonders. The creatures were looking for a way into her body, an entrance, some nod of recognition.

Fatma didn't know what to make of this. She could see a man standing over her, eyes wide and intense, shepherding the creatures back to their pages in the Book of Animals. Noor was there, too, watching her, whispering secrets about himself or the shepherd, she couldn't be sure: "My name is al-Jahiz—as if names would help you find your way in and out of my world. I have spent my whole life in books, looking for the River of Animals—that river and that river alone. There are many rivers and some of them travel in disguise. They cross my path and lead me astray, away from the one river I seek. I have drowned in their currents. But now I am here, now I am the river itself. So stand clear and make way for my flood and the bodies my floodwaters carry."

The man kept staring at Fatma. He looked down at a page in his book and raised his eyes to her again. Now there was a warning in his words: "This book was the road that I followed in search of the river. I gave my life to writing this Book of Animals, sacrificing my eyesight, any chance I had for human contact, and all the inks I could buy. I was looking for a river that I had all along. It's true—I traveled far and wide in search of something that already existed within the confines of my own self, my body—the Animal. It's all there in the book now— the river, myself. Do you imagine, if I allow you to wander freely in this book, that you'll be able to reach the headwaters of my river? I must warn you—it contains the essence of all creatures and their histories, including yours."

The more the man spoke, the more Fatma's feeling of pregnancy increased.

"Listen to your own story . . ." His words eddied around her like siege-weapons in love's eternal war.

There, in the book, Fatma saw herself taking on the shape of a green leaf. She, the leaf, was being carried by a man so beautiful he sparkled. This man, or spirit, flew through the sky cupping Fatma in his musky palm, and as he soared the leaf-greenness suffusing her body and soul gradually darkened.

They descended to earth, landing swiftly in an endless expanse of sand, and scurried toward a mountain that bulged like a frown on the brow of the horizon.

At that very moment, on the opposite side of the mountain, a traveler named Mohammed ben Himyar was striding up the slope. He had a treacherous serpent in his belly.

As the distance between Fatma and Mohammed ben Himyar closed, she became aware of the story behind the traveler's presence. Mohammed had been walking along when the snake in his belly, who was a Vengeance Snake, cut across his path looking for protection.

"Hide me from my enemy," the snake implored. "He is large and powerful."

"Come hide in the folds of my tent," Mohammed said.

"But my enemy would find me there—no doubt about it."

"Then come and hide in my cloak."

"He'd find me there, too."

"Then hide in the space between my rope and my skin."

"Oh no—he'd find me there."

"Well, you could hide in my body. But then you might kill me."

"God forbid. I won't harm you, I swear. May God be my witness."

Mohammed opened his mouth and the snake slithered down into his stomach. When the snake was sure her enemy had gone, she tickled the roof of Mohammed's mouth and announced her attention of injecting her venom directly into his heart, or maybe just eating his intestines.

"But you swore you wouldn't harm me," Mohammed protested.

"Fool! Just like the rest of your gullible race! When will you people ever learn?! I betrayed your grandsire Adam! Wasn't I the one who tempted him out of Paradise? How could you even begin to trust the likes of me?"

"Please allow me at least to go to the top of the mountain," Mohammed pleaded. "I'd like to build a gravemarker for myself there."

The snake granted Mohammed a little time to erect a gravemarker. With a sweep of his huge green hand, the spirit-man cleared the

way for Mohammed. When Mohammed told him about his predica-
ment, the spirit-man held out his hand and showed him the dark-
green leaf he was carrying.

"Eat it," he insisted. "Chew it and swallow it."

Mohammed chewed hungrily. As the Fatma-leaf mixed with his
saliva, it turned into rays of poison and light. When the Fatma-leaf
reached his belly, the serpent took one look at her power and fell to
pieces.

"Your silent prayer reached our court," the spirit-man told the
grateful Mohammed. "All the angels and courtiers sighed in sympathy, and I was chosen to come to your rescue. That green leaf you ate
was a leaf from Toba, the Mother of All Trees growing in Paradise."

◆　　◆　　◆

"It would be easy for you to trace your roots to that Mother Tree,"
Noor said. There was a teasing note in his voice.

"You mean I could be anything I choose?" Fatma asked.

"You can be the daughter of Toba, you could be Balkees, Queen
of Yemen. Or you could be invisible. It's all up to you."

"Can you imagine," Fatma asked, "how it feels to be a leaf, changing all the time—to be bolts of lightning and spears of venom?"

"Deadly poison?"

"Worse than that. To be all-powerful, to be absolute energy, to
have the power of infinite justice and revenge . . . it's a strange taste,
so many different tastes all in one, battling one another."

Fatma was in such an exalted state, so blindingly vivid, that Noor
became frightened. He crept silently back into the wall and closed
his book, releasing Fatma from her leaf-life.

"My husband says that I'm an idol made of *fertasya* stone," she
said. "What is he talking about?"

Her question gave the shadow pause. He slipped off the wall carrying a copy of *The Wonders of Creatures*, a book by al-Qazwene. He opened it and pushed one of the pages against Fatma's waiting fingers.

"The *fertasya* stone, if I'm not mistaken, was mentioned by Aristotle," the shadow explained. "It grows at the base of the tallest mountains. At nightfall it glows like a lantern, giving off bewitching fire and light. But when it's ground up and dissolved in celery-water, it turns into deadly venom capable of killing anything that comes in contact with it."

Noor watched the emotions drain from Fatma's face. "You could be that stone," he whispered, "if you choose. Or you could be the Philosopher's Stone that turns base metal into gold. It's all a game. You set the rules. You can play it any way you like."

"It's only a game?"

Touched by her uncertainty, the shadow leaned closer and looked deeply into her burning eyes.

"Actually, you remind me more of a pure yellow bezoar stone," he said, "the famous stone from the Western regions, the one that can cure vicious bites and draw off deadly venom."

♦   ♦   ♦

Sajir had returned a while ago. He stood in the open doorway staring impassively at his wife's nakedness as if she were an exotic specimen no different from one of the snakes. When he sensed that she was coming out of her reverie, he snorted to make her aware of his presence. She didn't move or look at him, but he could tell she saw him.

"You know, no matter how beautiful you become, there's not a man alive who could love you." His lips were tight, like someone forced to say what he was thinking. When he realized he wasn't going to get any argument from Fatma, he began to sound less strained, and

he continued with confidence. "No, there's not a man alive who'd let you near him. Someone sees you, they feel nothing, not even pity. If one of my clients picks up your scent in the poison I've sold him, he breaks out in a sweat. There's no way for the simplest human feeling to get through that serpent skin of yours. And just look at those snakes—they all know you and blindly obey you the way they submit to a storm or sickness or a catastrophe or the fact of death. These creatures know nothing of love or loyalty; they cling to your skirts only because they sense the evil in you."

Fatma adjusted her gauze robe, covering herself, and moved coolly past her husband, out of the room. Sajir squinted toward the snake farm. It looked empty and cold. The serpents glared at his trembling arms and legs. Suddenly he knew he'd made a mistake proclaiming his true feelings in their territory. He realized, too, that in all the time he'd known them, the snakes had been waiting for him to say what he'd just said, to break the truce or bond between them, so they could stop deferring to him out of respect for his family's profession. The serpents wriggled with ominous pleasure.

Fatma darkened her eyes with *kohl* and wrapped herself in a purply old skin so delicate it practically dissolved as she put it on. She set about cleaning the cages in preparation for nightfall. With her purple aura and heady scent of the ancient past, she adjusted the temperature of the room, banishing the chill that had disturbed the snakes, resettling them in warmth and silence. The last glimmer of dusk on the ceiling gave way to blackness, completing the day's cycle of light and covering the snakes with the darkness they wore like crowns.

"Make me a glass of tea," Sajir barked. He knew Fatma was busy, but he was more determined than ever to treat her as his slave.

With her customary noiselessness, she turned her back on the cages, went over to the stove, and lit a flame; it flared like a one-eyed animal. Sajir kept his eyes on her, especially on her hands. He was convinced that one day she was going to dip her fingernails in his drink and poison him.

He plumped a pillow on the old carpet, sat down, and waited. She walked over to him carrying the clear glass. The moment she set it down, he batted it away. The glass shattered, splashing tea on Fatma's left foot and spreading a dark stain across the carpet. She turned away without cleaning it up. Sajir grabbed at her blindly and dragged her down, groping her, fumbling to get inside her. Suddenly, when his fingers touched her thighs, he jumped back, the veins in his hands twitching in shock. He bit his tongue and collapsed on the carpet, breathing hard. The electricity shot through him in waves, keeping him paralyzed for some time.

Fatma stood up, still silent, and walked to the snake farm. She resumed her work with the serpents, feeding them dozens of insects and rats, but no stewed frogs. To the snakes' evening meal she added rare old seeds that increased the amount of poison they made, doubling their yield of venom and the volume of business Sajir was able to do. ("Toba's seeds" was Noor's joking name for this refinement in the snakes' diet.)

Sajir sat up without saying a word. He knew now that there was a point beyond which he could provoke his wife no further, or she would bring some unthinkable punishment crashing down on his head. He held his peace till she finished her chores. Then, when he couldn't stand another second of it, he slipped out of the house and joined the men sipping tea and gossiping out on the street. He sat with them but said nothing. He just sat there, mouth agape, the image of his wife's tattooed body imprinted on his eyes. He was intimidated by her newly enhanced powers; he knew she was in control of his world and his fate. But in a strange way he wanted her. He wanted to break through to her, needed to get through to her. Actually, he wanted to break her, smash every last bit of her to pieces, leave nothing unbroken. He wanted to crush her core, erase the inhuman scent of her. He wanted to leave her in ruins.

He sensed, however, that a species of impregnable flower was blooming inside her, enclosed in a protective shell, a bell-jar of serenity. He was torn between his feverish need to crack that shell and the unspoken truce they'd arrived at during their trip. Crossing the line with Fatma had become too risky, Sajir was sure of that much.

Fatma took no notice of her husband's seething; she was too busy attending the great rebirth happening in her body. Something was growing and taking shape inside her, she could feel it. She was swept up in a rising fever of joy and ripeness, bursting with the life force that had taken hold of her, swelling her body and soul, pulsing through her fingers and fingernails, struggling to emerge with every move she made. There was a near-narcotic sweetness to her breath and the husky timbre of her voice. She was a furnace of creation. She lived each moment for the very next one: she was going to have a child.

Sajir came back inside. The stain on the carpet had been cleaned up, along with the shattered tea-glass and the rest of the mess. Fatma was putting random stitches in her *abaya*, which seemed to be getting darker and darker.

Sajir stood there for several minutes, staring and trying to comprehend the invisible branches of Toba, the Mother Tree, whose black-green leaves were tumbling out of Fatma's *abaya*. She scooped them up as quickly as they fell and returned them to the silk. Sajir tiptoed off to bed and fell fast asleep.

By midnight, Fatma was panting with the effort of trying to keep up with the storm of leaves from the Mother Tree. The entire room was turning dark green. All the snakes in the snake farm gathered around her, braiding themselves into a triangle around the base of the Tree, their eyelids quivering as the Tree's vibrations moved through them. Fatma knew that Sajir must be suffocating under the thickening greenery, just as she knew that the flood of growth would sweep everything before it.

At daybreak, in an instinctive struggle to cling to his drowning existence, Sajir blinked. When his eyes came fully open, the scene vanished.

Fatma sighed. To Sajir, she looked quite small now, suspiciously so, bent over her *abaya*. He called out to her. Obediently, she put the black silk away and lay down on the bed.

He broke the promise he'd made to himself never to touch her again. He jumped on her, penetrated her immediately, battered her blindly, woodenly, jabbed at her. Fatma's newly healed wounds were tender; the pain was unbearable. She felt she was being torn to shreds.

Suddenly an edge hardened inside her, a sharp emerald blade between her thighs.

Sajir withdrew and rolled away in a flash, leaving her bleeding.

For the rest of the day she lay in bed waiting for him to attack her again. But he did not return. He was nowhere to be seen.

During the next three days Fatma did very little but shuffle between the snake farm and the bathroom. She wanted to wash the memory of the assault away, but her body was strangely reluctant. She stumbled around in a daze, unable even to focus on the simple task of bathing. The light emanating from her navel grew dim; her vivid memories began to fade, as did her willpower. She moved ever more slowly, as if coated with frost. Her dreams changed drastically.

Though she could not close her eyes to sleep, the images were as clear as ever: now it was Ibn Madhy rather than the knight who came to escort her. The old poet seemed to be familiar with the route she'd traveled earlier. Once again they climbed the slope of the dam. A stiff, icy wind shrieked in the darkness, spitting pebbles in their faces. Grimly, Ibn Madhy swatted them away; he was much tougher than mere nuisances. When they came to the colonnade at the top of the dam, the stone guard was still standing there, hacking away at the wind and the shadows with his three-bladed axe, keeping everything away from the doors.

Ibn Madhy turned to Fatma. "It is time," he said in an otherworldly whisper.

The knight appeared out of nowhere. The wind howled dementedly, seized Fatma's *abaya*, and tossed it in the air like a bird. Icy shadows swept across the key, clutching at it and freezing it into the silk—and freezing Fatma's soul in fear.

The hidden key went into action. The knight knew exactly where to look for it in the *abaya*. His strong, time-worn fingers passed over the silver threads in the *abaya*, the silk heaved, and the silver coalesced in the palm of his waiting hand. The knight did not let it lie there. Moving with the lightning-speed of a hero in a dream, he dodged the stone guard's axe and plunged the key into the center door. With a deafening hiss, the door cried out, scalding the lifeforms that clung to the rocks near the colonnade, turning the insects, trees, and tufts of grass a sickly yellow.

The doors collapsed. The colonnade and the mountain exploded. The knight disappeared in a dark shower of whizzing stones. Fatma saw Ibn Madhy being tossed against the nearby mountain of al-Sarwat, and in the place where he fell, she could see the wicked Fire Serpent beginning to move and spark with the flames that had consumed the martyrs in King Thonawas's ditch. The time had come for the great Serpent to show itself to the world.

Sniffing mortal air for the first time in many centuries, the Serpent stretched and thickened like a whip lusting for blood. It crept from village to village, burning steadily, never resting, cutting a swath across the sky from East to West, reversing direction at sunset, relentlessly seeding the land with death, leaving nothing but cinders in its wake.

◆   ◆   ◆

Fatma woke up. The stench of smoke was gone. The snakes were all quivering, listening to fading echoes.

Fatma dismissed her dream. But when she picked up her *abaya* and saw that the silver key was missing, her heart froze. With icy firmness, something told her that her adventures were over.

For three days she was unable to go near the water. The storm raged on inside her, keeping her paralyzed.

From the southern provinces came reports of terrible fires. Death was everywhere, spreading rapidly, heading north.

On the afternoon of the third day after her dream, Fatma was sitting by the flint basin in a stupor when the shadow inched away from the wall. Noor bent over her and tenderly began to wash her like a newborn baby, massaging her with pure essence of shadow, melting the frost from her limbs, relaxing her. His dark waters, his magic shadow-waters, flooded her, touching her more intimately than she had ever been touched. From the tips of her fingers to the depths of her soul she felt sated, fulfilled. A new feeling of calm came over her. She smiled a deep sensual smile, glowing with satisfaction. She felt at peace, whole again.

Noor's water, soothing and familiar as a lover's caress, soaked into her hair, untangling the twists in her braids, freeing her hair to cascade down her back, patiently stroking her skin like the fingers of a lover who wanted to know more than the all of her he already knew. The dark waters penetrated her skin and settled into the knots in her muscles, kneading, caressing, cajoling, drawing each tendon into flowerlike buds. Fatma stretched out in lazy ecstasy. Her heaviness slipped away. She felt cared for. And powerful. She felt one with the shadow—and now that she was a shadow, she saw herself clearly for the first time in her life, saw her beauty and individuality. She was able to see herself as a separate being, with the ability to stand back and take a good look at what she was. She beheld her other body, her spirit body, feather-light and free, and she experienced the incomparable richness of a soul transcending the pain of the moment.

She dozed off.

She was walking across a rock-strewn desert, somewhere near the tents of the Yamis. There, on the horizon, like majestic clouds hugging a sea of black stones, stood the green domes of their pavilions in all their splendor. She entered one of the tents and was immediately engulfed by dense greenness. There were no angry reds or yellows; even the figures who rose to welcome her were clad entirely in green, sparking green sparks. The men and animals hurried out to greet her as if they'd been waiting for her all along. Fatma sank deeper and deeper into the surging green sea.

Noor woke her up. She looked around, her eyes still blurred by a green haze. It took a moment for the green to recede and for natural color to return to the things in front of her eyes.

Noor regarded her with a strangely satisfied look on his face. He produced a copy of Ibn Seren's Book of Dreams, opened it to a section illustrated with towering green tents, and began to read:

"Being sheltered by such a pavilion, or living in one, is a symbol designed by the Guardian of Visions. Its purpose is to reveal the secret entrance to the land of ease and luxury. Green is the mask worn by the Messengers; green is the way to the fountains of pleasure. Green is the color of martyrdom. Green is your key to the secret gate, green is your companion." Noor's voice fell to a whisper. "Open your heart. Bare your soul. You're coming with me now."

Fatma remembered the words of their first conversation — "I want you to come with me." Was she hearing at last his final invitation to death? She felt no fear. The invitation, the key, and the road that was opening before her — it all felt so familiar.

◆   ◆   ◆

"The martyrs' ditch, the holocaust of King Thonawas, has come to life again," Ibn Madhy began. "And it is sowing death along all the highways and byways."

These were the words the old poet had used to lead the stone knight to the key hidden in Fatma's *abaya*. That is what he had meant by "It is time."

The knight returned to Fatma several times, seeking not the key but the fire burning within her. "It is time," he said over and over, trying to persuade her to follow him down the Great Serpent's road of flames and death.

Fatma knew nothing of the deadly fires plaguing the southern provinces. Increasingly, however, she was haunted by dreams in which she followed the knight, his stony soldiers, and Ibn Madhy to a battlefield, where they kept missing some decisive battle.

Fatma followed the trail of the Great Serpent without ever catching up with it. Her dreams were strewn with smoldering cinders and fire-blackened corpses, some of whom rose in an attempt to follow the Serpent. Fatma marched along with the corpses looking for the Thonawas-Snake. Dream after dream, march after march, she tramped from place to place, beating the earth to dust in desperation. It was exhausting, and there was no sign of King Thonawas's fire. Each repetition of the dream brought Fatma closer to a state of collapse. She turned almost transparent with fatigue.

The knight was turning darker now, dark as onyx. He had risen from his long sleep in the rocks in order to win this final battle. He set traps, he prodded the earth with spears, he coaxed it with magical mirrors. He searched in vain for the Serpent, for a place to take a stand against the Beast.

As for Fatma's sleep—as soon as she closed her eyes, the knight entered her dreams to enlist her in his elusive war against the Serpent of Thonawas.

Ever since Sajir's assault, she'd been conditioning her body by drinking water from the snake vat. It was scented with *kadi*, a plant that flowered only in the southern provinces.

◆ ◆ ◆

One morning Fatma was startled out of her dream by the sound of retching. She looked up from her bed on the floor and saw Sajir bent over double, his body blocking the door to the bathroom. She hurried to see what was wrong. She caught the acrid smell of vomit. She stood behind him, watching, wanting to stroke his back and comfort him, but he was tight as a drum and in no mood to be touched. Thick green vomit, the contents of his poisoned gut, was splattered all over the floor. She stood there waiting for him to do or say something.

He twisted around toward her. "Were you in the habit of entertaining visitors while I was away?" he asked angrily. Fatma didn't know what to make of the question. "I can't stand the way you smell," he said. "That musk is driving me crazy."

He raised his hands in a gesture of command. Fatma poured

water over them. Frantically, he splashed it on his face in an attempt to clear the ashen color from his cheeks and wash away the sickness tearing at his stomach. "Where do you get all that musk?" he asked. Fatma was speechless. He poked her in the ribs. "Where in God's name do you get it all?!"

A powerful whiff of musk filled the bathroom. Sajir retched again. Fatma waited patiently for the spasm to ebb.

"No," she said simply.

The lone word penetrated his pain. Weakly, Sajir raised his head. "Leave me alone, stay away from me. You're killing me."

Fatma walked to the snake farm, shut the door behind her, and started cleaning the cages. She raked the beds of sand with a fine comb, swept away the chill that had settled at the bottom, and removed the parasites that tended to collect there. When this was done, she ran her comb through the sand again, smoothing the pathways, manicuring the tiny sand-drifts and the shadows they made with the tip of her finger, so that the snakes' invisible life force would be free to flow as it pleased. With practiced skill she rearranged the buried images of the reptiles' ancient kingdom; now the unseeing creatures would be able to bathe in their timeless, once-upon-a-time splendor.

Fatma herself could see the Kingdom of Snakes, and the pasturelands of Najran, spreading over a distant part of the world known as the White Land. There, in universal whiteness, every snake was godlike, the creator of a universe unto itself. They slithered between the towers of the great city of Najran, vassals of the old king, feasting their eyes on the glorious whiteness and its palette of peace and beauty. White pasture lands lay around the city like rings of joy, endless shimmering circles scattering rainbows of images and light. The snakes, the king's subjects, basked in the beauty and drew nourishment from it.

The sand between Fatma's fingers grew warm. It began to glow; it was coming alive. Suddenly she became aware of Sajir standing in the door of the snake farm.

"Sniff the air," he said. "Even the snakes are beginning to smell like you. You must be setting some sort of trap."

Fatma poked a stick in the spot where the Great Horned Black usually nested.

Sajir kept his eyes on her fingers. "You haven't answered my question," he said quietly but forcefully. "Where do you get your supply of musk?" There was a finality in his tone; he was not about to be put off.

Fatma turned and faced him. "I've never had any perfume at all," she said rather meekly. "And I have no way of getting any—as you know."

"You expect me to believe that?" He burst out laughing, cackling insanely. "Yes, yes, of course, of course . . . most assuredly, my queen." He calmed down and glared at her. "Your courtiers are paying homage to your statue. They shower your image with perfumes and presents and all kinds of beautiful things. I beg your forgiveness, your majesty. How could I have been so stupid?"

He bowed elaborately and left the house.

◆　◆　◆

The crescent of the new moon rose over Mecca. Sajir began searching the house in a frenzy, looking for the source of Fatma's musk. He turned the carpets upside down and upended all the pots, but found nothing. Furious as he was, he didn't dare come near the cages. Though he knew that every stick of wood and grain of sand might contain a fountain of perfume, his madness was such that he could only run around in circles. Vomiting became part of his daily routine. It was almost as if he'd come to enjoy gagging on the air itself and retching at the very thought of his enemy. He took demented pleasure in flaunting his revulsion for the kingdom from which he'd been exiled.

8 *The Revolution*

One night Sajir, numb and detached as ever, came to his wife's bed. Fatma was dreaming about a sacrifice, an amber idol, and the violet flames of the Yami ravaging the land. She was walking in search of King Thonawas's Serpent. . . . She heaved breathlessly.

She opened her eyes to see Sajir's masklike face looming over her. His hands were fumbling at the bed clothes. She watched him as he stripped the covers from her legs. He was being very careful not to make contact with her lethal skin. He raised himself up high and penetrated her.

Fatma's body made a decision on its own: Her muscles convulsed, becoming hard as emerald, and gripped his sword. He drew back in shock but was unable to pull out. The Nurse's soft feminine sinews had taken control, ignoring Sajir's curses and threats, and Fatma's own surprise. She was as helpless as he was.

"Let go of me!" he hissed. He grabbed her thighs and punched them. "Let go of me, you animal!" In a rage, he punched her in the stomach. He kept hitting her, kept trying to weaken her with the methodical iciness of his anger. In twenty years of marriage, this was the first time he'd allowed his real feelings for her to show. Fatma remained strangely cold, hard and strong as obsidian.

Sajir realized he was trapped. He was naked before his wife, with no mask to protect him. He lost control of the demon within himself. The demon howled and kept hitting Fatma, to no avail.

With a superhuman effort he managed to pull himself, even as his body convulsed, out of bed. Fatma was still connected to him, knotted groin to groin. With another mainstrength effort he dragged the two of them to the bathroom. Fatma was stiff as a stone. Sajir turned on the water tap, and steam began to rise in the suffocatingly small room. Fatma tried numbly to get away, but he yanked her savagely under the faucet, exposing her naked back to the full force of the hot water. She spasmed, releasing him. A preternatural shriek shook her soul.

Sajir was crying. She had no idea what might have happened to make him weep so violently—she was the one who'd been scalded. But he, for some reason, was writhing on the floor clutching his groin. "I, the Nurse, must have broken his sword," she thought.

It took Sajir some time to get his torment under control. The second he was able to stand, he threw Fatma out of the house and out of his life. Now he was safe in his hiding hole.

The shocking (though not quite surprising) thing was how swiftly such a calculating man, after twenty years of smug assurance, managed to act. It *was* surprising, though, after twenty years of complete acquiescence, how ferociously Fatma's body had turned against him.

◆　◆　◆

Reports of deaths in the southern regions increased. More and more, Fatma dreamed about those southern lands. She was still searching for the Serpent of King Thonawas. She sensed it was growing larger every day. But it kept eluding her, exhausting her. Day and night she dreamed of the Serpent, and the dreams were eating her alive. The walls of the temple of her body were becoming so transparent that one could see the scaffolding of her bones.

9 *How She Lay Dying on the Porter's Bench*

atma was totally disheveled when she arrived on the porch of the Yemenite porter's house. Her skin had turned so pale that the black miniatures stitched into her *abaya* seeped into her, making marbled veins that bloomed against the whiteness of her skin.

To the old porter she looked very old, like an ancient piece of onyx from Yemen. Onyx had long ago stopped meaning very much to ordinary people, and its curative properties had been forgotten. Nevertheless, it could cure the most grotesque deformities, for onyx was the Stone of Beauty.

Fatma was oblivious to her own deathlike pallor. She surrendered to her condition as if poisoned. She was dissolving into the patterns of black and white created by her skin and her *abaya*.

As for the Yemenite porter, his left arm and the palms of his hands had been contaminated by contact with the *abaya*. They were turning into onyx, a very soft, nearly alive sort of onyx.

Fatma knew she was dying. She knew there was no other way back to the shadow, to Noor. But she was afraid of returning to the flint trough because she was sure she'd find no trace of her secret companion. Still, her years of secrecy and dissimulation had come to an end; she stood naked before her fate. All that remained to be done was to go his way, death's way. To go under . . . under . . .

144

◆   ◆   ◆

"All your beauty, all your vitality . . . going to waste, turning into dust, into nothing . . ." The Yemenite porter was overwhelmed with grief so profound that he, too, looked old beyond his years.

"I'm going to a world where I'll be able to show my true face," Fatma said. "Part of me has already gone on ahead to the invisible world. I can be myself there, I can be truly alive."

"And when you do show your true face," the Yemenite said, "would you come back to me and let me have a peek at it? I'm an old man, you know; I don't count the years anymore. Most of them were the same anyway. I could be a hundred, for all I know. I've lived my whole life as a stranger. I left my happy home in Yemen and came here—God knows why. I never had a chance to make a life for myself, never even touched a woman. Cleaning buildings—that's been my only passion. Now the buildings are falling apart. I've lived more of my life with stones than with flesh and blood. So I suppose it's a kind of reward for you to come and die with me."

◆   ◆   ◆

Fatma closed her eyes and drifted away with the haunting, floating murmur of Noor's voice. It seemed to rise out of her own body. The shadow was about to recite the poem he had been promising to read her.

"Listen to this poem about the road that opens before you." The sound of his voice was bewitching as he turned the pages of the Book of Heaven, and the scent of basil, hanging in the Yemenite's porch, drifted into Fatma's soul.

"The queen parted her lips," the shadow began. "A tunnel, a gallery of light, opened, stretching all the way to a great throne rising

in the Unseen. On all the roads beautiful travelers stood waiting to hear the queen breathe her last. And when the last breath escaped the crumbling temple of her body, the queen was wrapped in basil soft as silk, and her body was passed from traveler to traveler, to all the travelers who aspired to the Unknown, and as they journeyed from heaven to heaven, each of the seven heavens opened its gates before the queen's shroud of basil, and the travelers who stood in attendance took the shape of prophets and angels and sacred cocks beholding the basil and saluting its scent.

"At last the queen came to a curtain of pure light. Her shroud trembled as if drawing breath. The intoxicating scent of musk was everywhere. The queen's breath took on a life of its own and became a body of scented light, which in turn became a spell that raised the curtain of light.

"As the curtain rose, the throne was revealed. The queen's breath quivered and emerged from its womb of basil and materialized as a lovely column of calligraphy, and the column bowed before the throne.

"The letter-column found its place on the page that the great King was holding in his hands. All the word-worlds on the page heaved a sigh and revealed their secrets to those who could see, and in less time than it took to know what was happening, the differences between all creatures were dissolved, and all became one with the ancient, eternal worlds. Those who approached the throne were charged with a powerful glow suffusing all of creation."

Fatma felt her body falling away. She was ready to enter the book.

"It's time," she said, her lips fluttering as if kissed by a breeze.

"It's time," the Yemenite porter repeated, hypnotized by Fatma's sweet whisper.

◆   ◆   ◆

It occurred to her that someone ought to know she was about to die. The news of her death should at least be made known to the courtiers in her decaying kingdom.

Fatma made her way to her husband's apartment and knocked softly on the door. He answered and stood there blocking the entrance.

"I'm dying," she said.

"Well. . . ?" He did not close the door.

Though he showed no reaction, Fatma could tell he believed her. He continued to stand there, covered only by a sarong draped around his waist. Beneath the garment she could see his emerald blade and the violet sword fringed with violet death. Sajir was death-in-life.

She staggered to the stone bench, covered herself with the exquisitely embroidered *abaya*, crumpled, and died.

Her corpse heaved. A black larva emerged, a magnificent serpent of blue—or purple-black, with many other colors iridescing on its surface. The serpent moved away from the onyx corpse, the temple of Fatma's body, and stood facing it.

Fatma knew at once that her fire had come out of her body. It neither burned her nor horrified her. It was simply her; it was her genuine self.

She was summoned to the southern regions by Ibn Madhy. The old poet, himself a flame-larva, witnessed the emergence of her flame and made ready to mingle his fire with hers. Together they headed further south.

The old Yemenite sat on the floor, propped his feet against the legs of the stone bench, and expired. His face was serene; he looked more like a guard in death than he ever did when he was alive; he was a statue that had acquired great solemnity and strength. And in an oddly captivating way, he looked younger and even darker.

Back in the snake farm, everything suddenly went cold. It took no more than a second for the temperature to drop to the freezing point. The whole room was coated with dull gray cobwebs of frost.

No matter what measures Sajir took, the room remained frozen. He tried lighting a fire in the flint trough, but as soon as he pulled his match away, it sputtered and died. Heat had been exiled from the snake-shrine.

The snakes were paralyzed. When Sajir touched them, they crumbled and turned into infinitesimal gray motes that floated away in the air. Sajir was trembling when he approached the viciously beautiful cobra, one of his late wife's recent discoveries. Tenderly, pathetically, he touched it, only to see its breathtaking colors and patterns lose their shape and fade away. The deadly reptile literally disappeared. In just a little while, there was not one snake left.

Sajir was ruined—he had lost all his snakes; his fortune was no more. The vicious, pitiless brutes had left him to follow their mistress, who was surely a witch. Even the shadow had been erased from the wall of the flint trough. And now, all of a sudden, the flint itself turned into volcanic stone, blackened as if by a smoldering fire. All color, all joy, drained from the room.

Teeth chattering, Sajir stepped outside, closed the door and leaned against the wall, utterly desolate. The cold pawed at him through the door, through the walls. The whole house was icing up. He clenched his teeth. He was rooted to the spot, a statue made of glass, becoming more and more brittle in the cold. The cold crept into his soul and his memory, and soon he lost what little awareness he'd ever had. One after another, the compartments in which his past was stored fell to pieces, leaving his mind naked before the world. It was as if an army of snakes had swept through his brain and blotted out every breathing memory with their secret inks. The invisible serpents removed from his storehouse all knowledge of their habits and needs, and everything he knew about the remedies that could be concocted from their venom. He lost all feeling for how to catch snakes and how to care for them. He was a stranger to them now, and every fang was a threat.

◆   ◆   ◆

It was the finest death Fatma had ever experienced. She was a snake of the purest ebony black. Every creature in the world found a place on her skin. For the first time in her existence, the Nurse was moving through the very heart of life. Her dream of the *al-Zamel* dance was coming true.

With the speed of lightning, she moved in the direction of the great Serpent of King Thonawas. Along the way, her retinue encountered the army of her husband's demons, hissing and sparking in the distance, doing their best to bring her fire under control. The Yemenite porter was all around her, everywhere at once, eager to take part in his queen's transformation.

From under the branch of a nearby tree, buoyed by the wind, flew a winged dervish. The dervish uprooted the label "Nurse" from Fatma's memory. A bolt of lightning struck the ground in front of her. On the edges of the jagged line sketched by the lightning bolt, Noor was waiting, his shadowy form suddenly alive with spirals of words, rivers of words, words exquisitely drawn in musk and saffron. They overwhelmed her senses, opening doors she'd never imagined, leading her to places she'd never dreamed of knowing and loving. Curtains of light rose before her, and as the curtains rose her soul grew lighter, bursting with pleasures so intense she could not name them. By the time the seventieth curtain began to rise, she was a whiff of perfume on Noor's currents of love, a deep, all-powerful love whose force Fatma could feel now as surely as flesh.

The sensation was of being securely held. The holding was fulfillment.

She could see her own image everywhere, and Noor's too. He was simply a reflection of her inner self. She felt complete, she felt everywhere at once. Her fire-soul was soaked with water, and the water was the powerful water of life and love. Now, once and for all time, she was whole, a river of water dissolved in fire, flowing everywhere.

Just as Fatma came to this realization, the Serpent of Thonawas appeared. It was feeding on the burning hot ocean of sand surrounding her, raking the earth with voluptuous swaths of fire, sweeping whole cities and villages into the void.

Suddenly the earth heaved underfoot and Fatma was carried off to a place where she stood face to face with the devastating fire. There, on a mountaintop in Najran, Thonawas recognized her at once. They clashed, fire against fire, sparks flaring, blackening the sand all around them. Water sprayed from the sparks. As the battle continued, the sparks turned to fountains of water. The serpent that was Fatma took on the shape and power of the stone knight who had led her to the top of the dam.

Fire against fire, water against fire . . . the devil Thonawas weakened. Finally he was destroyed—completely, eternally defeated.

Fatma-Serpent flowed on, a river of water and light. She was the River Lar, coursing through the Arabian Peninsula and carrying with her, in endless gliding images, every living creature. And bodies whose substances were dreams.

Balkees, Prince Taray, Taray's soldiers, and his fine white camels were there; Ibn Madhy, Ibn Sakran, his silver falcons and gazelles— all were there, patiently waiting, flowing. All were the River Lar. All were everlasting.

AFTERWORD

My Thousand and One Nights

In May of 1997, my wife, Wendy, and I and our eighteen-month-old son, Michael, traveled to the Kingdom of Saudi Arabia, to Jidda, the port of entry for nearly three million pilgrims who make their way to Mecca every year. Wendy had been invited by the USIS to conduct photography workshops for Saudi women. I was to give lectures about American movies and literature at King Abdul-Azzis University. We arrived, cultural baggage neatly packed, just as the heat of the desert summer was coming on.

In the visible realm, there is very little that is old in Saudi Arabia. During the oil boom of the eighties, Jidda was completely rebuilt in the style of a sprawling mall-city in Arizona. There are not many amusements unless you enjoy hanging out at McDonald's or Burger King. While Wendy kept busy with her workshops, I swam with Michael in the poaching-temperature pool or rolled his toy truck up and down the driveway, which was paved with marble, as were the floors of the many malls we visited.

We stayed at the home of the American cultural attaché. The final night of our stay, we were invited to dinner by two women who'd been taking Wendy's workshop, Raja Alem and her sister Shadia. Raja was well-known in Arabic literary circles as the author of six novels, several plays and numerous collections of poetry. Shadia was an accomplished painter. Most remarkable for women in the Kingdom, the sisters were unmarried. They had founded a Montessori-like school where they taught for ten months a year. Afternoons they spent talking about the past with their aged father, a retired government functionary whose memory was failing. Once their father fell sleep, Raja wrote and Shadia painted. During school vacations, they traveled to Cairo or Beirut, which they'd received permission to do after lengthy wrangling in the courts. They had visited France and England, but had yet to see the United States.

A driver brought Raja and Shadia to our house. As the sisters loosened their *abayas* in the privacy of the living room, I caught a flash of western jeans. Raja was in her mid-thirties, Shadia a couple of years older. They were tall and slender, with muscular agricultural wrists and dark, fathomless eyes. They were twinlike in their tenderness and vigilance toward one another.

We fell into diplomatic banter about whether to go out for Chinese, Italian, or Middle Eastern food. Raja and Shadia preferred Chinese, but when my wife protested that we could get Chinese food in the States, it was agreed that we should try a restaurant serving local food.

"Our car will take us," Shadia said, buttoning her *abaya*. "It will cost one thousand dollars an hour."

"No problem," I said. "You're a fabulously rich Saudi."

"And you're a fabulously rich American," Shadia replied.

Wendy and the sisters settled in the back of their seventies Oldsmobile; I sat up front with the driver. We drove north on a highway bordering the Red Sea, past the high-rise apartments that had stood empty for ten years, ever since they'd been offered rent-free to Bedouins who preferred their tents to twentieth-century accommodations. We arrived at an open-air restaurant: starlight, refreshing breeze. The maitre d' greeted Shadia and Raja familiarly. Music brayed from the loudspeakers; evidently we were beyond the reach of the religious police. A few days earlier, when I'd taken my son to an amusement park, I'd been struck by the absence of music, which was frowned upon by Saudi Islamic law.

We settled on couches facing the waveless sea and passed the hookah around. Shadia turned in my direction like a soft statue. "By the way," she inquired, "would you happen to know any American publishers interested in Saudi Arabian novelists?"

Though her sister lacked the bilingual fluency of Joseph Conrad or Samuel Beckett, she'd written her latest novel in English — literary English. "But I don't know how I *sound* in English," Raja said wistfully.

It was quite a feat for a Saudi woman to have written anything at all and to have had her writing published. Having accomplished this, Raja still faced the unscalable wall standing between women and society-at-large. She had decided to try to reach beyond the wall.

I scanned her manuscript during the long flight home. At times her prose resembled Proust's, but oddly rendered in classroom French — dense, mesmerizing, and syntactically mangled. Stylistic considerations aside, its substance was a revelation after the oppressively blind days I'd spent in Jidda.

Though I'd written a couple of books and done a bit of journalism, I made most of my living as a cinematographer, and years in the camera trade had sharpened the instincts that drove me to see what I wasn't supposed to see, and under no conditions to be shunted aside. The oppressiveness of Jidda I took as a professional affront. Here at last, in Raja's manuscript, was a chance to *see*.

I was unable to read the manuscript without paraphrasing as I went along, so I wrote down my "translation" and faxed Raja the first fifteen pages, adding an apology for my presumptuousness. The next day she faxed back corrections and clarifications, and said that she was embroidering my initials in Arabic script on a bolt of black velvet so that she would be able to cast Bedouin spells appropriate to the task I had undertaken. She stipulated that in order for the spells to be effective, she needed to know my mother's unmarried name, which I instantly supplied.

A typical passage in Raja's original went like this:

The rivers answered her longing, roaring down the mountains. . . . The Najrani people echoed that roar with their owns. Hundreds of colorful men were lined in the roads, performing Al-zamel dance to salute the leaving guests. Line after line of glowing daggers and flowered heads ebbed and flowed. The dancers moved according to the rhythm, flowing behind the gathering-speed truck. Females in black adorned with silver and red she-camels which flowed with the hypnotizing drums. The hundreds of hair braids matched camels' saddles adorned with endless red, yellow, and silver braids. Fatma saw the endless lines following on the receding road, following and flowing in her dreams all the way to the city of Mecca. Taray's last words haunted her, he was there in her black silk, the way he came to her that last night, the way they found him.

This became:

The rivers, answering her desires, ran faster, foaming. The people of the village cheered. The roads were jammed with brightly robed men dancing *al-Zamel* in honor of their departing guests. Behind them stood row upon row of swordsmen and women, flowered headdresses bobbing. The snake truck gathered speed. The dancers highstepped after it, trailed by women in black, silver anklets jangling, and still more women in yellow gowns, others in flowered skirts— and behind them, swaying to the pounding of the drums, came the camels, silver-braided saddles jingling, echoing the bouncing braids of hundreds and hundreds of women. From the back of the truck, in what seemed an endless reverie, Fatma watched the crowd of Najranis recede like a backward-flowing river rushing toward the holy city of Mecca, so far away. Taray's parting words still rang in her ears. He was with her now, here, in the black silk of her *abaya*, as he had been with her that night, as he was when they'd found his body.

My knowledge of Arabic literature was limited to *The Arabian Nights*, the famous collection of stories that have their origins in pre-Islamic campfire tales. Which is to say that my knowledge of Arab writing and its mischievous narrative strategies was equivalent to knowing that Shakespeare is a dead Englishman who wrote a play about a confused prince. Deliciously overwhelmed, I groped along, leaving nothing out, improvising where it felt right, swapping faxes with Raja—earnest faxes about the futility of transliterating Arabic names, giddy faxes about dreams and oil prices and the weather—and doing my best to convey her blend of delicacy, high seriousness, and sensuous density. Along the way I got to know a few of her secrets, and Arabia's.

In countries such as Saudi Arabia or India, where mother tongues are regarded as dialects and where an airless sort of English serves as the *lingua franca* of the educated classes, it is natural to assume that one is communicating when using words as basic as man, woman, water, thirst, death, food, sun, home. In fact, one is communicating merely a sketch of the mysteries denoted by these words. One is "speaking translation," a language so neutral it has no life of its own, a dialect as suspect as Switzerland.

This thicket of half-comprehension gets denser when translating a writer like Raja. Her vision (to play shamelessly on the title of Edward Said's book about Western myopia regarding Islamic lands) is dis-Orienting. What are we dealing with here? An anthropological curio? A philosophical tract in the form of a Harlequin romance? A *fotonovela* without the *fotos*? A message in a bottle, the finding of it more disquieting than the message?

Years ago, while socializing with Mayan glyphologists in southern Mexico, I learned a valuable lesson. After several late-night tequilas, one of the glyphologists confided that the very, very, *very* strange Mayan graphics (elaborately feathered people lancing their tongues and penises with catfish spines and spilling rivers of blood, etc.) had long been assumed to be something practical and respectable, like calendars or astronomical charts. Then, in the early 1970s, Mayan studies came to be infiltrated by graduate students who brought along their generation's penchant for mind-altering substances. Under the influence of these drugs, especially LSD, the students were able to see that the Mayan graphics meant simply what they said. What they said and how they said it, however, were blended in a way that made it hard for Westerners, with our bias for linear literacy and compartmentalized sign-systems, to accept. The result of the young students' novel research methods was a lasting breakthrough, not just in translation, but in cross-cultural comprehension. My point, without insisting that psychedelic substances are an indispensable aid to appreciating Raja's work, is that it helps to open one's mind—really open it, unpack it, and leave it open.

Even with the purest intentions, though, it is impossible to resist the urge to transpose *Fatma* to a familiar key—to Disney, say. After all, Raja's art, like Disney's, is an art of ornate surfaces in the service of a few unvarying themes. It is innocently attached to its—what?—obsessions, and it makes a strong case for finding the resolution to life's problems in magic kingdoms. And what about those mind-reading snakes, those goddesses bursting into flames? One could, in the interest of blowing even more cultural smoke, proceed from Raja to Disney to Japanese animé, thence (to chase my own favorite smoke ring) from Japanese animé to Dante. Raja's métier, like Dante's, is part poetry, part cosmology, and authentically religious in a way that is scarcely comprehensible to us anymore. She believes not just in different things, she believes in them differently. She accepts The Invisible as a fact, as another realm of life, not fantastical but subtly veiled, like the dark matter which many cosmologists believe composes 90 percent of our universe.

Okay, okay . . . so there's really nothing close to Raja nowadays. You'd have to go back to Christopher Marlowe, or all the way to Ovid, to find anything so methodically lunatic and insistently lyrical. (Ironically, Raja's nearest kin in English letters may be Sir Richard Burton, in his over-the-top rendition of *The Arabian Nights*.) Such comparisons are useful as far as they go, but they tend to discount the moral striving that underlies Raja's *mise en scène*, and it is this, as much as her lyricism, that has made her the preeminent artistic voice of her place and time.

Which brings us to the character of Fatma and the matter of why it can sometimes be so difficult to extend her our fullest sympathies. Fatma, for all her torrentially passionate imagining, seems very much an innocent captive feeling her way around her cell. Depending on our squeamishness about the atrocities which our own neighborhood of society visits on its least esteemed members, we may be so appalled at the conditions of her captivity that, in an inversion of the Stockholm Syndrome, we come to disapprove of the captive herself, or condescend merely to pity her.

In the end, Raja's work might best be approached like a treasure chest full of costumes, masks, and veils. You could, if you like, study the designs, classify them, and puzzle about their possible meanings. Or you could just try them on, page by page, veil by veil, and revel in their beauty.

◆　◆　◆

Early in the morning of September 11, while searching my e-mail for something from Raja, I saw the headline announcing that a plane had just crashed into one of the World Trade Center towers.

The last I'd heard from Raja was a couple of months earlier, when she'd e-mailed me from Vancouver. She'd written about how much she and Shadia enjoyed bicycling through the forested hills around the city and hinted at the possibility of moving permanently to Canada. It had been more than a year since I'd translated *Fatma*, and in that time Raja and I had finished another novel and had embarked on an autobiographical story about her childhood in Mecca. And once, while the sisters were passing through New York on their way to visit relatives, we enjoyed a hectic afternoon together, scampering from museum to museum and, in what I insisted was the essential New York experience to be savored in the brief time available, standing squashed together in the East Side subway during rush hour while I pressed on Shadia an urgent request to lower oil prices. "Oh you Americans!" she said. "Always so self-centered!"

"I don't mean *American* oil prices," I replied. "Just lower *my* oil prices, okay, please?" It was cozy and fun, like our literary collaboration. Now, with the towers burning and civilians dying, and no word from Raja, I felt a cold panic. I needed to know that somehow we were still together. Two weeks passed; the wounds of 9/11 festered, the world drifted toward more bellicose imbecilities. Still no word. In one final attempt to reach her, I quit trying to explain things or ask for anything and just e-mailed her, without comment, a passage from *Haza Haza Haza*, one of the novels we'd worked on, the story of a blind dervish named Dawood:

Dawood stayed with his speckled camel, who was heading north, leaving the caravan behind. The wind gusted, scattering pebbles in his path. The ravines and gorges were steep; there must have been great seas here at one time. The cliffs soared so high that no sunlight touched the pits and valleys forking far below.

The speckled camel snorted a charming dromedary song. Dawood was harmonizing in a higher register when he caught sight of a caravan far more spectacular than the one he'd left behind, lurching and stutter-stepping along a narrow mountain path.

Though their identities were well concealed, there was no mistaking the camels for anything but purebreds. By cunning and prayer, the deserts of Arabia had long ago perfected the ungainly beasts of rude pastoral times; nowadays purebreds of high intelligence were taken for granted. Still, the specimens standing before Dawood were worthy of serving in the temples of the gods.

The camel drivers were clad in pale purple-blue robes patterned with silvery tiles and tassels of pure silver and cowrie shells. Dawood thought of the treasures in the riverbeds and shallows ringing Arabia. The silver seas and the rivers of light flashed in his mind, tempting him back to the time before The Great Fire, to that appallingly long day when the sun came too close to earth and scorched its face with a flame so brilliant that it turned Arabia's Eden into barren desert, leaving only the beauty of its dunes and the groping of the sun on the sand to insist, with stunning clarity, that this Eden had once been loved, but loved too warmly for Paradise to endure.

Raja replied at once from Jidda. She and Shadia had been ma-
rooned in Paris for several weeks, she said, without access to e-mail.
They managed to get on a plane to Saudi Arabia after being ordered
to wait for hours in line with other suspicious-looking people of color.

I am home. But where under the sun is the place we can call home?
I feel that the whole earth, the entire universe, is home.

I don't know why I cried when I read the lines you chose from
Haza Haza Haza.

From September 11 on, the only thing I thought of was you,
Wendy, and Michael. I was not at all worried about you; you seemed
just to float in my mind like grand pictures, no words or thoughts,
just you in your garden watching the ever-changing colors, or praying. I've always depended on those prayers.

We are perplexed, not knowing where we stand in all this. The
New York that was hit, does it belong to somebody? Is the Louvre a
French treasure? The first time I came to New York, I was shocked
by those giant buildings. The human beings who created them
seemed trapped in their beauty and ruthlessness. I thought, you
could hardly see the sky from the streets. The rain had to fall
straight down in order to reach you, otherwise it would have to stay
in the sky.

I immediately thought of *Haza Haza Haza,* I don't know why. I
do feel we have been pushed into a world where there is no place for
such a dream.

Death does not frighten me—you've come to know this about
me. Death is all around us, all the time. It is the human imagination
that is frightening. That's why I feel writing is the only way out, the
only way to transcend.

What made you think of those lines from *Haza Haza Haza?*

Yesterday, in the London airport, the Customs officer asked: "How long are you intending to stay in London?"

"We are not staying, just passing through, we are catching our flight to Jidda in an hour."

"So you are going back home?"

The question shocked me. Am I really flying home? What is home? But I felt, yes, I am going back home, truly—to the comfort of those eyes, the trusting eyes that know you for the dreamer you really are. There, you don't need to prove anything to anybody; you will not be threatened or accused. Home is where you can be yourself.

There have been times when I've called you from airports, from London or Paris. But not this time, when everybody was rushing to catch a plane after waiting in endless queues and being stopped by machines and hands greedily roaming your body looking for an instrument of death.

Yes, we are home.

Dear Sisters,

I'm writing quickly, wanting to reach you before Bush speaks on CNN.

When I was a kid in Brooklyn, before the Trade Center was built, I used to sit on the stoop of my parents' house and on clear days I'd gaze northward toward Manhattan and the Empire State Building shimmering like a heavenly castle on the horizon twelve miles away. Not very many years later, when SoHo (a neighborhood less than a mile from the World Trade Center) was still just a dilapidated nineteenth century industrial slum, I moved into a loft on West Broadway. The previous tenant had been a manufacturer of little souvenir Statues of Liberty. The floor was scorched where the molds had leaked hot metal. I lived there for sixteen years, raised my daughter there. From the roof I watched the Trade Center Towers being built. Though their arrogance wasn't pretty, they seemed another heavenly castle, with the difference that now, as a grown man, I was close enough to embrace them. I loved the sparkle of their lights at night and the way they anchored the city to the sky.

Of all the beautiful pages in *Haza Haza Haza* and *Fatma,* the pages I sent you remain my favorites. Ever since I translated them, I've kept a copy taped to the wall in front of my desk. I sent them to you because I want you to know that you are two of the most important people in my life, that my life would not feel complete without you and Shadia. The lines about Dawood and the speckled camel have always assured me that this world is beautiful and fragile. It assures me, too, that our world is loved, as the Eden that once was Arabia is loved, even though this Eden, the Eden we all desire, has been loved unto destruction.

Your brother, Tom

In the early days of our collaboration, I flattered myself that I was going to rescue Raja—in retrospect a genuinely flabbergasting assumption, rather like flattering myself that I could speak for her. She doesn't need rescuing, and I don't speak for her. I am privileged to speak *with* her. Since translating so many of her moonrises over Mecca, I will never see my moon the same way again.